Miracle at Augusta

A list of titles by James Patterson is
printed at the back of this book

JAMES PATTERSON
& PETER DE JONGE

Miracle at Augusta

CENTURY

1 3 5 7 9 10 8 6 4 2

Century
20 Vauxhall Bridge Road
London SW1V 2SA

Century is part of the Penguin Random House group of companies whose
addresses can be found at global.penguinrandomhouse.com.

Penguin
Random House
UK

First published in Great Britain by Century in 2015

www.randomhouse.co.uk

A CIP catalogue record for this book is available from the British Library.

Hardback ISBN 9781780893723
Trade paperback ISBN 9781780893730

Printed and bound by Clays Ltd, St Ives PLC

MIX
Paper from
responsible sources
FSC
www.fsc.org FSC® C018179

Penguin Random House is committed to a sustainable future
for our business, our readers and our planet. This book is made
from Forest Stewardship Council® certified paper.

To Sue, second-best player in our house
—JP

For my brother William
—PdJ

Miracle at Augusta

1

"ON THE FIRST TEE...from Winnetka, Illinois...the 1996 winner of the U.S. Senior Open...Travis McKinley."

I've never set foot on Augusta National before, let alone teed it up, so for thirty seconds, I just stand there shivering and let the polite applause of the patrons wash over me. Okay, "wash over me" is a bit of a stretch. How about "trickle over me"? Could you live with that? While the clapping subsides, I close my eyes and picture the shot I need to hit.

Because my grandfather gave me a book on the Masters one Christmas, I happen to know that Augusta was originally a nursery owned by a Belgian horticulturist named Prosper Berckmans. That's why all the holes are named after trees. The first, Tea Olive, is a 445-yard par 4, which doglegs left and calls for a high fade to the right side of the fairway some 290 yards away. When the image of the shot is locked in my mind, I step up and launch my drive into the December gloom, aiming twenty feet right of the big wire net that keeps balls from flying into the parking lot of the CVS next door.

I'm happy to report that my tee shot comes off pretty much as planned, leaving me 165 yards to an uphill green, so I swap the driver for my 7-iron and aim for the right rear corner of it. When the ball lands softly and trickles—like that applause—toward the pin, tucked up front, just beyond the trap, I give myself the eight-footer for birdie and move on to the par-five 2nd, aka Pink Dogwood.

My body may be fifteen miles outside of Chicago, freezing its nearly fifty-two-year-old ass off at the Big Oaks Driving Range on Route 38, but in my mind it's in Georgia in April, and those color-corrected dogwoods and azaleas have old Prosper turning over in his grave.

The start of my third year on the Senior Tour is a month away. As some of you may recall, my rookie year went rather well—unkind sportswriters leaned heavily on the word *miraculous*—culminating in my win at Pebble, which the starter was gracious enough to mention. My sophomore season, however, was lackluster at best, so I'm doing everything I can to prepare for '98, particularly since the shelf life out here is so brief, what with me growing more decrepit by the day and fresh young blood bubbling up from below. If you think it's hard fighting for scraps left by Hale Irwin, Gil Morgan, and Hank Peters, and believe me it is, imagine what it will be like next year when Tom Watson, Lanny Wadkins, and Tom Kite flash their birth certificates and step up to the senior buffet.

I don't even want to think about that. I just know that this year is huge, and since the end of October, I've been at Big Oaks every afternoon, fifth stall from the left, chewing up these nasty rubber mats and whatever cartilage is left in my right elbow.

To relieve the tedium, I've been playing virtual rounds at Augusta, hole by hole, Flowering Crab Apple to Carolina Cherry, seeing if I can find the correct half of the fairway and then land it on the correct quadrant of the green. Along the way, I try to keep my scuffed range rock from rolling back into Rae's Creek or finding the pine straw or nestling up behind the Eisenhower tree. It keeps me sharper than mindlessly banging balls.

For the front side, the nine they never put on the air, I make do with the pictures and descriptions in my old Christmas present, but for the back nine, I have thirty years of TV viewing to draw on. When I get to 12, Golden Bell, that nasty par 3 at the end of Amen Corner, I even know which tree Byron Nelson used to look at to decipher the swirling winds. Instead, I gaze roofward and see if there are any plastic bags whipping around in the currents. My favorite holes are 13 and 15, Azalea and Firethorn, the two short par 5s that have been the scene of so much drama. In the last couple of weeks, I've even been working on a high draw to keep it on those slippery greens, which, in my mind at least, are never less than 13.2 on the Stimpmeter.

Today, at 15, I catch it solid off the tee, and since I get even more roll off the Big Oaks cement than I would from the hard, sloping fairways at Augusta, I've only got 215 left, a perfect yardage for my new pet draw. As I prepare to launch the ball into the azure sky, there's a bang behind my left shoulder. It sounds like a shotgun blast but is in fact a shank from Esther Lee, the housewife in the stall to my left.

"Sorry about that," says Esther, raising a hand in a pink glove.

"No problem," I reply. But the reverie is broken, and suddenly it's a lot harder to pretend I'm in Georgia and not a drafty warehouse in suburban Chicago. After a couple more swings, I pack it in for the day and deposit my bag in the closet behind the front desk, where the manager has been nice enough to let me keep it, seeing as I'm here five days a week.

Then I drive the nine miles to Winnetka and get in line with all the other trophy housewives and husbands and wait for Noah to be released from his kindergarten classroom at Belltown Grammar. Elizabeth and Simon were already well grown when Noah made a surprise appearance nearly six years ago, and as I watch the little gink shuffle out of the back, his backpack hanging off one shoulder and his baseball cap turned backwards, I appreciate how lucky Sarah and I are.

"Hey, Noah, how was your day?"

"Not bad. How about you? How was Augusta?"

"Shot thirty-two on the front."

"Give yourself a lot of eight-footers?"

"You know what I say, Noah?"

"Charity begins at home."

"Exactly."

Our house is less than five minutes from the school, and seeing Sarah's Cherokee in the driveway makes us both uneasy.

"Mom's home early."

"Yeah."

When we get out of the car, Sarah is standing in the doorway. "I have some sad news to share," she tells us. "Pop died."

2

AT 2 P.M. THE FOLLOWING Saturday, some two hundred of my grandfather's friends convene in the parking lot of the Creekview Country Club and follow him up the frozen first fairway. By now, Pop has been reduced to the ashes that fill the Tupperware container head pro Matt Higgins holds in the crook of his left arm. When Higgins reaches the first green, he pulls off one glove, pries open the lid, and sprinkles a bit of Edwin Joseph McKinley over the portion of the green where the hole is generally cut.

As the gray soot rains down on the winter green, Higgins utters the signature words with which my grandfather started a thousand rounds: "No gimmes. No mulligans. No bullshit. Let's play golf," and the ragtag army, some of whom have been forced by age and infirmity to ride golf carts with home health aides, hurl it back in unison like a battle cry: "No gimmes! No mulligans! No bullshit! Let's play golf!" Then Higgins hands Pop off like a football, and another volunteer takes the lead.

It's an impressive turnout, particularly considering it's fourteen degrees. Included in the boisterous band of mourners is my best friend and former caddy, Earl Fielder, who came up last night from North Carolina. No doubt my grandfather would be touched to see so many dear friends. Pop, who hated slow play, would also appreciate the brisk pace. In forty minutes, the procession covers thirteen holes, and with five left, the next two generations of McKinleys take over.

Simon, a freshman at Northwestern, leads us up the par-five 14th. He carries his grandfather over the longest hole on the course, then turns him over to his proud younger brother, and now the chilled brigade, many of whom have been fortifying themselves with frequent nips from their pocket flasks, fall in line behind a five-year-old. After Noah guides them to the 15th green, they take particular delight in the unlikely spectacle of a kindergartner leading them through another chorus of "No gimmes! No mulligans! No bullshit! Let's play golf!"

But it's the McKinley ladies, Elizabeth and Sarah, who get to me the most on this freezing afternoon. Elizabeth, because she is surely the most devastatingly beautiful radiology resident in North America, and Sarah...because she's Sarah. Sarah walks off 17, she hands off Pop with a kiss, and it's up to me to carry him home.

Affection for my grandfather is inscribed on every face in this unholy procession, many of whom are by now overfortified, but for me the affection and appreciation are overwhelming. Without my grandfather, I have no idea where, or even who, I'd be. I wouldn't be a golfer. When I was eight, he put a cut-down 7-iron in my hand, and for the last forty-three years or so he's been my only coach. And when Leo Burnett tossed me to the curb a couple of Christmases ago, he was the only one who didn't think my grandiose scheme of qualifying for the Senior Tour was insane. I've been so dependent on his guidance, on and off the course, for so long, I'm more than a little worried how I'll do without it.

I carry Pop the final third of a mile and sprinkle what's left on 18, banging the bottom of the container like a bongo to make sure every last particle of the beloved man has been set free.

"No gimmes! No mulligans! No bullshit!" I shout. "Let's have a drink!"

"I think he means an indoor drink," says an old friend, turning over an empty flask, and we file into the clubhouse for one last round or three on Edwin Joseph McKinley.

3

AFTER EARL HAS RUN a gauntlet of McKinley hugs and kisses and accepted pats on the back and best wishes from a dozen of my grandfather's starstruck old cronies, I walk my friend from the clubhouse into the freezing Midwestern night. At the end of the flagstone path, a cab is waiting to take him to the airport, and as we approach the car, I realize, and not for the first time, that I also owe a great debt to Earl, without whom I never could have succeeded in my rookie year, and although I feel the urge to finally thank him in clear and explicit English, I fall short, in the finest male tradition.

"Thanks again for making the trip" is about the best I can manage. "As you can see, it meant a lot to all of us."

"It meant a lot to me too, Travis. When you kick off, I'll come to yours, too."

"Promise?"

"Yup."

"Thanks."

"See you in a couple of weeks, then. You ready?"

"I better be. I've been working my ass off."

"Good. Because I don't want to embarrass you out there."

When we've exchanged as much of this as we can stomach, Earl gets into the car, and I walk to the back of the lot and get into mine. After letting the heat run for five minutes, I pull up in front, where Sarah, Elizabeth, Simon, and Noah pile in.

Creekview Country Club is an older course and, like a lot of older courses, is in the center of a neighborhood that has deteriorated over the decades. On the way back to the highway we pass a series of strip malls, lined with liquor stores, pawnshops, and mini-marts that seem particularly threadbare on such a raw night.

In the last year and a half, I've done pretty well, almost embarrassingly so, and my one indulgence has been this Mercedes sedan. Although I've had it six months, I often still feel uncomfortable behind the wheel, an impostor, but the one time I never regret the purchase is on a night like this, when it's stuffed with McKinleys and I feel that, at least for the duration of the trip, the tanklike vehicle is protecting them all, not just from the wind and cold but from all life's other harsh realities as well.

Plus, as Noah often points out, it's kind of swank.

Up ahead, at the light, a broken-down old van sits on the side of the road. As I wait for the light to turn, a middle-aged woman climbs out of the driver's seat to gauge the extent of her problem, and when she walks in front of her car, we make eye contact. I know I should pull over, but the lateness of the hour and the sketchiness of the neighborhood lobby against it, and before I can offer a convincing counterargument, the light turns green and the impregnable Benz rolls on.

Two stoplights later, my conscience gets the better of me, or maybe I just feel the heat of Elizabeth's gaze on the back of my neck. "I'm going to circle back," I say, more to myself than anyone else. "See if I can help her."

It's a four-lane road and half a mile before I can make a U-turn. By the time I get back to the woman and her van, I'm relieved to see that a second just as beat-up car has pulled over and parked behind it, and an older man, African-American with a gray beard, is wrestling a spare tire onto the right rear wheel. I roll down the window and the cold air rushes in.

"Need any help?"

"That's okay," says the man, taking in the well-dressed family from below.

"Sure?"

"It's just a flat tire, sport. We got it covered."

4

IF THERE'S A BETTER place to spend mid-January than Hawaii, let me know. Till then I'll have to make do with Waialae Country Club on the island of Oahu, where Earl and I are getting our last reps in before tomorrow's start of the Azawa Open and warming our bones in the tropical sun. It feels so good to be warm, and out of that stall at Big Oaks, I'm hardly bothered by the fact that fifty people are lined up on the range behind Earl, and two are watching me, one of whom is my new caddy, Johnny Abate. Earl's fans, who have taken to calling themselves Earl's Platoon, aren't content to stand and gape. Every time he pures another 4-iron, they ooh and ahh and shower him with love.

"This is your year, Earl!"

"Hell yeah, buddy."

"You're the man, EF!"

And my personal favorite—"Earl Fielder is EFing good."

"I guess they don't get out much," I mumble under my breath to the object of all this adulation.

"What makes you say that, Travis?"

To clarify, I should probably point out that Earl has enjoyed a dramatic change in fortune since caddying for me in my rookie season in '96. For starters, he is now a member of the Senior Tour himself. He earned his playing privileges by finishing second in the '97 Senior Q-School, then backed it up with one of the most consistent rookie seasons ever, ending the year with twenty-three straight top tens. But what changed everything and transformed him into a bona fide celebrity is that Reebok commercial, which juxtaposes Earl on tour with old footage and photos of him from the late sixties in Vietnam. No one is happier for Earl than me, but do I find the clamor for autographs and photographs at restaurants and airports just a wee bit annoying?

Of course not. I'm a bigger person than that.

"Work on anything in the off-season?" I ask.

"Just tried to tighten everything up a notch. Keep the arms and body more attached, have it all move in one piece."

"Jesus, Earl. You already got the most buttoned-up swing out here. To get it any tighter you'd need a monkey wrench." But as Earl stripes a couple more, I realize he may actually have succeeded. Watching Earl, his broad forehead beaded with sweat, is like watching an Old World Italian mason build a wall. There's no wasted motion. Every move and gesture is pared to the nub.

"You're striping it better than ever, Earl, and that's saying something. You're going to get that win this year, maybe two."

"I wouldn't bet on it," says Earl. "I'm too much of a grinder. I may not stink it up, but I rarely go real low, either. Don't roll it well enough. But I'd trade all those seconds and thirds for one win. And not just for the exemption. I want something to be remembered for, and once you get your name engraved on silver, it's hard to get it off. How about you, Trav? You work on anything up there on the tundra?"

"See for yourself."

I pull my 5-wood, aim my club face and feet slightly right of my target, and as I swing, I focus on keeping my hips turning and really letting my arms go, ripping down, through, and up. The ball takes off with the usual trajectory but, a hundred yards out, shoots up like a rocket when the afterburners hit. It bends slightly to the left before landing softly 215 yards away.

"Son of a bitch," says Earl. "I need to see you do that again."

I dislodge another Titleist from the pyramid-shaped pile, nudge it into place beside the long, shallow divot, and turn on the ball one more time.

"Well, I'll be damned. The high fucking draw. The suavest shot in golf. I just have one question."

"What's that?"

"Why? There isn't one hole out here where you'll need it."

"It's for Augusta."

"Augusta?"

"How else am I going to keep the ball on those reachable par fives, thirteen and fifteen in particular? Those are birdie holes, Earl. You're not birdieing those, you're losing half a stroke to the field."

"I know that, Travis. You're not the only one with a TV."

"You get reception down there?"

"How the hell are you going to get an invitation—steal it from Tiger's mailbox?"

"Haven't thought that far ahead. You know it's a mistake to get ahead of yourself in this game. I just have a feeling I'm going to need it."

5

THE DISPARITY IN STATUS between Earl and me is reflected in our Friday tee times. Earl goes off in the early afternoon with Chi Chi Rodriguez and Raymond Floyd, and I slip out at 7:03 a.m. with senior rookies Trent Smith and Elliot Brody. I hadn't heard of them either, until I looked them up in the media guide. Smith joined the navy out of high school. Back on dry land, he sold insurance, ran a nightclub, and repaired pin-setting machines at a bowling alley, then spent fifteen years in Grand Prairie, Texas, in the auto repair business. He got into the field by Monday qualifying. Brody, who earned his spot through this year's Q-School, was a teaching pro outside Tacoma for thirty years.

It couldn't be a more congenial group. One look at each other and we knew we were all just slightly different versions of the same person—three guys who hadn't seriously considered making a living at competitive golf till it was almost too late, and now we're determined to make the most of our chance. What little chatter there is, is collegial and supportive, each of us giving the others the chance to do their best.

The setting isn't half bad, either. With no one in front of us, I feel like I washed ashore in paradise and just happened to find my sticks here waiting for me. The only sounds are waves, rustling palms, and birds. If anyone had gotten up at dawn and wandered over, they would have seen some quality golf. Among the three of us, we carded one bogey and fourteen birdies. All those sessions at Big Oaks must have paid off, or maybe it's the novel thrill of hitting off organic material, because six of those birdies are mine. For the next four hours, my 66 makes me the year's top player on the Senior Tour, and when the last player walks off 18, I'm tied for second with Gil Morgan, one shot behind the leader, Hale Irwin.

6

FRIDAY, I WENT OFF in the first group of the day. On Saturday, thanks to that 66, I go off in the final one. Instead of playing under the radar with two fellow journeymen, I'm trading shots with the two best fifty-somethings on the planet—Hale Irwin and Gil Morgan. Last year, Irwin won nine tournaments and more money than any golfer in the world, including an elegant young cat named Tiger Woods. Morgan won six times and earned more than Tiger, too. The last time I felt this out of my league was the summer afternoon in college when I got it into my head to play pickup basketball at a playground on the South Side of Chicago.

Everyone knows about Irwin, the former all–Big Eight cornerback with three U.S. Open titles, but it's the late-blooming Morgan who is the revelation. For one thing, he possesses a perfect swing. Literally. When he was a kid, his father, a small-town mortician, took him to see Harvey Penick, the legendary Austin pro who taught Ben Crenshaw and Tom Kite. Penick took one look at Morgan's move and sent him home. Said there was nothing he could do for him.

Irwin's swing is not nearly as lovely and he's much shorter off the tee, but he possesses a level of competitiveness and confidence that is borderline psychotic. As impressed as I am that Morgan hits it twenty yards past Irwin all day, I'm even more impressed by the fact that Irwin could truly not care less.

I don't want to belabor the point, but here's one last illustration of the chasm in golfing prowess between me and them. Last year Irwin led the tour with an average score of 68.93, and my average was a shade under 71. In other words, if we had a regular game at Creekview Country Club on Sunday mornings, he would have to give me a stroke a side. But at Waialae on Saturday afternoon, I didn't need any strokes from anyone. When our round is in the books, I've carded my second straight 66 to Irwin's 69 and Morgan's 70.

Those aren't typos. That's just golf.

7

FOR THE FIRST TIME since that U.S. Senior Open I keep bringing up, the name McKinley looks down from the top of the leaderboard. And it's in excellent company. Sharing my lead at six under are two of the best players and biggest personalities on the tour—Lee Trevino and Hank "Stump" Peters. As the patron saint of golfing long shots, Trevino has forever occupied a special place in my personal pantheon, and the thought of going off with him in the final group on Sunday is thrilling. But seeing that Hank Peters will be playing with us makes my stomach hurt.

You know how some competitors always bring out your worst? Peters has been providing that invaluable service for me since he beat me on the eighteenth hole of a college match when we were juniors, him at Georgia Tech, me at Northwestern. At the time, Northwestern was the kind of school a powerhouse like Georgia put on the schedule to pad their record, and that was one of the reasons I wanted to beat him so badly. Another was that Peters, an all-state quarterback in high school, exuded exactly the kind of big-guy swagger that has always stirred my darkest competitive instincts, probably because at 6'2" and 137 pounds, I exuded something quite different.

In our first encounter, back in college, I was two up with three to play, yet Peters never for a second thought he would lose, and of course he turned out to be right. After he knocked in his winning putt, which thirty-two years later I still recall as an uphill twelve-footer that broke two inches to the left, he shook my hand and said, "You got a nice little game, son. Stick with it."

"Thanks, Hank."

I guess there's something about being condescending, patronizing, *and* better that leaves an indelible impression. Then again, I've always had a talent for nursing slights. I collect them like a wine snob collects Bordeaux. I never know when I might need to dust one off. Not that this one has been paying dividends. Since I got out here, I've been paired with Peters three times and gotten drubbed every time. Maybe it's because I try too hard. More likely, it's because Peters, who won eleven times on the regular tour, is better and always will be.

On Sunday afternoon, Trevino comes out sporting four shades of brown—beige cashmere sweater, light brown shirt, dark brown slacks, and darker brown shoes, and just watching him work his way through the crowd with his distinctive slightly bowlegged gait makes me smile. Peters arrives wearing a camouflage hunting cap and sweatshirt, with several pinches of chewing tobacco stuffed between his teeth and lower gum, but for some reason I find his version of populist charm less endearing. My expression must give me away, because Johnny A promptly walks over and puts his hand on my shoulder.

"Now, listen," he says, "we're not going to let this cracker take us out of our game."

8

EASIER SAID THAN DONE, when this particular cracker has been living in my head rent-free for three decades. Trevino plants his tee, doffs his cap, and busts his iconic open-stanced move. His flat, abrupt chop—somewhere between martial arts and grunt labor—produces the same low, hard fade it has a million times before and ends up smack in the middle of the fairway.

"I hit that sunnabitch quail high," he says to his adoring gallery. "But I guess there aren't a lot of quail on Oahu."

After ejecting a brown stream of tobacco juice into a Styrofoam cup, Peters knocks it ten yards past Trevino, who at fifty-eight has lost some distance. Appropriately enough, I'm up last, and as I go through my routine, I can sense how anxious the gallery is for me to get it over with so they can hustle down the fairway and watch Trevino and Peters hit again.

Nevertheless, I catch it solid and roll it past them both. Having hit the longest drive, I'm last to hit again, and this time the gallery doesn't even pretend to wait. Halfway through my backswing, the scenery shifts like the furniture between acts of a play. I yank an easy wedge ten yards left, and when I fail to get up and down, I walk off the first green with a bogey.

"Only the first hole," says Johnny A. "Plenty of golf to be played."

True enough. And on the par-three 2nd, I hit my 6-iron to fourteen feet. Knock it in, I'm back to where I started and it's all good. Unfortunately, I'm so eager to undo my opening bogey, I charge my birdie putt five feet past and miss the comeback for another bogey, and on three, I'm so pissed about one and two, I bogey that as well.

Bogey. Bogey. Bogey. Not exactly the start I had in mind, and while I'm barfing on my FootJoys, Peters and Trevino are keeping theirs nice and clean, carding two birdies each. The round is barely fifteen minutes old, and I'm five strokes behind and well on my way to another traumatic defeat at the hands of my outdoorsy, tobacco-juice-spittin' nemesis.

At this point, I should summon my inner Lombardi and dig deep, but God knows what I'd dredge up. Instead, I relax and watch Trevino. For all I know, I'll never get a chance to tee it up with Super Mex again, and if I can't enjoy it, maybe I can learn a thing or two.

The first thing that stands out is the way Trevino parcels his concentration. Yesterday, Irwin and Morgan never peeked from behind their game faces. From the handshakes at the first till they signed the scorecards in the trailer, they never stopped grinding. Trevino has a different MO. For the thirty seconds it takes to plan and execute his shot, he and Herman are as focused as assassins, but once the ball stops rolling, they go right back to shooting the breeze, picking up the conversational thread—dogs, Vegas, barbecue—wherever they left it, as if trying to win a golf tournament is a minor distraction from an otherwise carefree afternoon.

And if the conversation lags, or we're waiting for a green to clear, as happens on 5, Trevino walks to the edge of the nearest hazard and fishes out balls with his 7-iron. He reminds me of my cheap buddies back home, except that Trevino tosses his plunder to the kids in his gallery.

I'm so captivated by the rare opportunity to observe Trevino in his natural habitat, I barely notice my own birdies on 7 and 8, and when I'm looking over my eagle putt on 10, the prospect of sinking it is such a nonevent, I roll it dead center from forty-five feet. Now I'm back in the hunt—two behind Peters and one behind Trevino—

and the thought of evicting Peters from my brain is so tantalizing, I immediately start pressing again.

On the next seven holes, I give myself legitimate birdie looks on five and never scare the hole. Surprisingly, Peters and Trevino can't make anything either. Over the same stretch, Peters misses three putts shorter than mine—I guess legends and assholes aren't immune to pressure either—and we head to 18 exactly as we stepped off 10, with Peters one up on Trevino and two up on me.

9

THE PAR-5 FINISHING HOLE is a gauntlet of palm trees, mined by bunkers, which I avoid and Peters and Trevino don't. That means they have to lay up, and I have a chance to reach in two.

Johnny A paces off the distance to the nearest sprinkler head and checks his yardage book. "Two fifteen to the center," he says, "two twenty-nine to the flag."

As soon as that first number falls out of his mouth, I smile involuntarily, because it's a number close to my heart, the perfect distance for my new high draw that got me through the winter. Of course, as Earl was unkind enough to point out on the range, the high draw offers no tangible advantage, and since this isn't figure skating and there are no points awarded for degree of difficulty or artistic expression, there is no sensible reason to pull it out now. Except one. If I go with the high draw, I just might be able to foster the illusion that rather than coming down the stretch with Peters and Trevino on Sunday afternoon at Waialae, I'm back at Big Oaks on a Tuesday morning with Esther Lee. And maybe, with a little luck, I can sustain the illusion long enough not to choke my brains out. Plus, as even Earl concedes, it's the suavest shot in golf.

When Johnny A hands me my 5-wood and says, "Nice soft cut, center of the green," I don't bother to contradict him. Instead, I do what I did all winter...in reverse. Instead of savoring the reality of this Hawaiian paradise, I transport myself eight thousand miles away to a drafty, underheated warehouse in the midst of a brutal Chicago winter. The breeze rustling the palms? That's traffic whooshing by on Route 38. The waves breaking on the shore? Trucks rattling over the potholes.

I do such a thorough job of conjuring those chilly practice sessions, my biggest fear is that Esther will shank another one in the middle of my backswing. It's a feat of reverse double psychology that might not impress mental guru Bob Rotella, but when my ball drops softly on the green and settles fifteen feet from the hole, it impresses the shit out of Johnny A.

"I thought we said high cut. But let's not split hairs."

It also makes an impression on Trevino. "Golf shot, Travis," he says, and I swear I'm not making that up.

"Thanks, Lee," I respond, and I would have been more than happy to carry on back and forth like this for another ten minutes, but seeing as he and Peters have their second and third shots to contend with and I've got some work left on the green myself, I reluctantly cut our conversation short and follow Johnny A to the green.

10

WHEN WE GET THERE, I discover I'm even closer than I thought, which is always nice. It's more like thirteen feet from the hole, and considerably closer than Peters's twenty-one feet and Trevino's eighteen. And they're lying three.

If you watch televised golf—and if you're reading this, that's more than likely—you've heard that pros never root against their competitors. You believe that, I have a warehouse conveniently located on Route 38 you might be interested in. When Peters attempts his birdie, I'm pulling so hard for it to miss, I may have given myself a hernia. If so, it's worth a little outpatient surgery, because his putt stops three feet short. Trevino misses too, although I swear, I wasn't bad-vibing my pal Lee... at least not as much.

Once they tap in, I've got those thirteen feet, a McKinley dozen, to force a play-off with Peters. Thirteen feet is no gimme. It's about three gimmes. But it's manageable, the kind of putt even I can stand over with a certain level of optimism, if not confidence, and Johnny and I are taking our sweet time / stalling, if only to get my heart rate down. Although our extended deliberations must be boring the crap out of Trevino and Herman, I know Peters is watching. For the first time in thirty-two years, I may have his full attention.

There is another reason Johnny A and I are taking our sweet time / stalling, and it has nothing to do with the enormous consequences or the fact that there is enough mental baggage between Peters and me to fill an airport carousel. The putt is dead straight. As long and hard as Johnny and I stare at it, we can't see any break, and the last thing a pro golfer wants to see when he squats behind a putt is nothing. *Nothing* is spooky. *Nothing* messes with your head.

Canvass a hundred guys out here, ninety-nine will agree. On a crucial putt of this length, they'd rather see two inches either way than nothing at all. A dead-straight putt is like looking at a mirror with too much light. It reveals way more about you and your stroke than any pro wants to share with himself, let alone his rivals. Then again, a lot of the people in that survey would say I'm barely a pro at all, which may help explain why I pour it dead center.

11

IT WOULD BE AN exaggeration to say that when Peters climbs out of the cart at 11 for the start of our play-off, he's a broken man. That's asking too much. But he's clearly dispirited by the recent turn of events, just as I'm buoyed by them. For the first time in our unhistoric rivalry, which may be a rivalry only to me, I'm the one feeling jaunty.

You can see it in my step as I hop from my own cart, and my uncharacteristic bonhomie as I chat with Marcus Azawa, chairman and CEO of Azawa Enterprises, the sponsor of the tournament. Judging from my social ease with him and his vice president of marketing, you might conclude I'm employable. And when I pump Peters's hand for the second time that afternoon and wish him, with utter lack of sincerity, good luck, there's a few extra pounds of pressure in my grip. I'm feeling so ebullient,

I'm half tempted to ask Peters if he can spare a pinch of Skoal.

Eleven is a shortish par 4 with water left, and based on the numbers we draw from the chairman's palm, Peters has the tee. That's another break for me, because it gives him that much less time to recover from his disappointing finish. He closes his eyes and inhales deeply through his nose, trying to delete the memory of those missed short putts, but unless your last name is Woods or Irwin, that rarely works. As soon as Peters hits it, he knows it's wet, and when it dives into the hazard, the Azawa Open is mine to win or lose.

Now I'm the one taking New Age breaths. Before Peters's ball has reached the bottom of that man-made lake, Johnny A has pulled the 3-wood from my hand and replaced it with a 4-iron. Somehow I keep it dry, and Johnny and I head up the right side of the fairway while Peters trudges up the left. He takes his drop and hits it about thirty feet left of the hole, and I hit my 6-iron about the same distance to the right.

On the green, the lengths are so close, it takes a rules official and a tape measure to determine that I'm far. Since we're on the same line, that's a break for Peters, but I still like my chances. If I can lag it close and tap in for par, Peters will have to sink his thirty-footer to tie.

Unlike 18, this putt has all kinds of break, at least four

feet of break from left to right, but Johnny A and I are far more concerned with the pace, since the last thing we want to do is run it eight feet past or leave it five feet short. On lag putts, my grandfather taught me to feel the distance, not just see it, and as I walk back and forth between my ball and the hole, I process the contours of the green and the route my ball will travel, through my feet.

"Weight. Weight. Weight," whispers Johnny A when he finally hands me the ball, and as I place it in front of my marker, I repeat the message to myself like a mantra. My first practice stroke feels a hair tentative, the second a tad strong, and when I put the putter behind the ball for real, all I'm trying to do is split the difference.

The contact is solid, and the weight feels right. And even though we didn't grind over the line anywhere near as much as the speed, I got that right, too. Six feet from the hole, as the ball slows, takes the breaks, and swerves inexorably toward the hole, I know it's in.

12

WHEN THE BALL CATCHES the high side of the hole, my putter is already in the air. It glints in the sun like a saber as the ball drops from sight, and it's still pointing heaven-ward when the ball catches the back edge and comes flying out the low side twice as fast as it went in. (See *physics: gravity; centrifugal force; the combination thereof.*) When it stops rolling, I'm ten feet from the hole.

I appreciate that only Jack Nicklaus has earned the right to lift his putter when the ball is four feet from the hole, but I've never hit a better lag in my life. Ever. My only mistake was being too close on the line. Ten inches left or right, I'd have a kick-in par, but because I missed by a fraction, I've got ten feet.

Even worse, I've given Peters hope. Now he doesn't *have* to make. Despite his dunking his tee ball, two putts will likely extend the play-off, and one could end it. Since

I've given him such a good read, he steps up and lets it roll while the line is still fresh in his mind. By this point, I'm too exhausted and traumatized to risk another hernia. I just turn away and glance at Johnny A...until the crowd explodes.

I've got to give Johnny credit. He doesn't bat an eye. "You already hit one good putt," he says. "We need one more."

He's right as usual, old Johnny, and it's shorter than the one I just made on 18. But that feels like a year ago, and I'm not the same golfer as the one who sank that putt. I wouldn't recognize that guy if I were sitting next to him. I tell myself not to hit the putt until I'm ready, but that could take a week and I doubt the networks would go for that. When I can't put it off any longer, I step up to the ball and give it a roll. It's not even close. Peters, that son of a bitch, is going to be living in my head for the rest of my life.

But wait. It's not over. First I have to watch two beautiful beige-skinned Hawaiian girls in grass skirts prance onto the green, kiss Peters on each jowl, and anoint him with red leis. As I'm enjoying this lovely native ceremony, Dave Marr, the on-course reporter, comes up from behind me, lays a consoling hand on my shoulder, and asks me to tell the viewers "how I feel."

"Like puking," I say. "And please take your hand off my shoulder."

13

FOUR HOURS AFTER PETERS hoists his crystal pineapple, Earl and I are lifting filthy shot glasses at the horseshoe bar of the Ding Dong Lounge, a gritty dive on the border of Honolulu's red-light district.

"This place is even better than I remembered," says Earl.

"That's the beauty of dives," I say, "they improve with age."

"Just like you and me, my friend."

We toss back our shots and chase them with cold beer.

"To the Ding Dong," says Earl.

"Long live the Ding Dong."

"Fuck. I'm amazed it lived this long."

After Earl heard what happened in sudden death, he felt duty bound to get me hammered as quickly as possible, and after five shots of Jameson and four cans of Primo, which I'm told is the Pabst Blue Ribbon of Hawaii, we're making solid progress. And since neither one of us sees any benefit in being photographed stumbling onto the curb at closing time, he thought we'd be better off in an obscure hole-in-the-wall than one of the glittering tourist traps near the hotel. Then he remembered the Ding Dong Lounge, first visited almost thirty years ago on an R&R trip during his second tour in Vietnam.

Despite my gloom, the Ding Dong had me from aloha. From the gentle, murky light to the pleasantly dank aroma to the scarred wood surface of the horseshoe bar, everything about it is imperfectly perfect. Halfway through my fourth Primo, even the name starts to grow on me.

"I know it was a sad occasion," says Earl, "but it was great to spend a little time with Sarah and the kids. You're one lucky motherfucker. And not just for being born white."

"Luck has nothing to do with it," I say with a straight face.

"Oh, really?"

"Survival of the fittest. Natural selection. It's science, really. But speaking of luck, I've got to say, I didn't feel so goddamned fortunate four hours ago when that putt caught the lip on eleven and..."

Earl puts down his Primo and points an admonishing finger. According to the ground rules for this excursion, clearly laid out on our walk from the hotel, any reference to "ancient history," as in what happened on the golf course this afternoon, is strictly off-limits. "The goal," he said, "is not to understand it, which would be impossible anyway, since it's golf, or even to learn from it, but to forget it, or at least dilute it."

"You're right," I say, getting back on script. "I'm a very lucky Caucasian. Lucky. Lucky. Lucky. Although I'm not sure Sarah feels the same way."

"How could she, under the circumstances? But let's take your kids. You know how many turn out to be assholes? A lot. Yours are smart, decent, and fairly good-looking."

"Thanks, Earl."

Earl reaches for his Primo, and in midsip, his eyes go slack, like he just saw the ghost of an old army pal who didn't make it home.

"You okay?"

"Not really," he says and, with the same blank expression, mumbles more to himself than me, "Motherfucker...of all the joints, in all the towns, in the whole motherfucking world, this motherfucker walks into mine."

When I swivel in the direction of Earl's empty gaze, I

see that three large, beefy men have joined us at the bar, and that the one in the middle is wearing a red lei.

"Hey, Travis," says Peters. "Hey, Earl."

Although his greeting could not be more innocuous, it causes his two friends to double over with laughter. All three are at least as intoxicated as me and Earl. Why shouldn't they be? They have something to celebrate.

"Hi, Hank," responds Earl for both of us.

"Travis," says Peters, "I got to say something. For the record. What happened on eleven was the worst piece of luck I've ever seen." And when I don't respond, he adds, "No shit."

"I know, Hank. I was there. Remember?"

"We're grown men here, give or take. We've seen lipouts and power lipouts. But this was another level. A tsunami to a hurricane. Your ball came out the other side like Dale Earnhardt coming out of the five turn at Daytona."

Peters, to my surprise, has a gift for simile.

"It was like one of those putting machines some asshole executive has in his office where the ball goes up a little ramp and when he makes it, there's a bit of a pause before the thing spits it out. Then the ball rolls down the little ramp back to his loafers, the kind with little tassels on them. And then his hot secretary sticks her head in the door and goes, 'I got Chandler on the horn. What

42

should I tell him?' 'Tell him what you always tell him, doll face—I'm busy.' You know the kind?"

"Yeah, Hank, I think I do."

"Why am I telling you? You were in advertising. You probably had one."

In the last couple of minutes, his friends have managed to regain their composure, but now beer comes flying out of their mouths and they slap the bar.

"Could we talk about something else? Believe it or not, I'm actually trying to forget it. As a matter of fact, that's why we're here."

"I mean, what the fuck was in that hole, Travis? A snake? A frog? And one other thing, what was your putter doing in the air?"

I still hear their laughter, but now it seems far away, as if reaching me from a distant room, because at this point I'm out of my chair and flying through the air toward the red lei and his giant jug head. Even in midair, I'm aware of having crossed a line from which there is no graceful retreat. As soon as I reach Peters, I have no choice but to start punching, and Peters has no choice but to punch back.

14

THE SPORTS BAR BETWEEN Gates 7 and 8 in the American Airlines section of the Honolulu International Airport is no Ding Dong Lounge. There's the antiseptic airport smell and the barrage of highlights and scores blaring from overhead TVs—does a twenty-seat bar really need four televisions?—but my biggest issue is with the light. There's so much glare bouncing off the tarmac, I'd need sunglasses even if I didn't have a black eye.

A respite from the noise induces me to glance upward. ESPN has gone to a commercial and there's Earl, three miles outside of Hanoi, walking in his new Reeboks, over terrain he used to hump in combat boots. Now he's talking to some elders in a village, sharing photographs of himself as a young soldier, and now he's standing beside some rice paddies doing a clinic for the kids as a water buffalo looks on. I hope it doesn't end up as a pair of golf shoes.

When *SportsCenter* resumes, I take a sip of my Bloody Mary and assess the damage. In addition to my shut right eye, which is more purple than black, all the ribs on my left side are sore, and one may be cracked, because when I raise my left hand to push my Ray-Bans back on my nose, there's a piercing pain. That must be why I'm drinking with my right. In addition, my head hurts in a way that can't be explained entirely by a hangover.

Nevertheless, I don't feel bad. On the contrary. Sixteen hours after the fact, the thrill of having survived and almost held my own in a brawl with camo-wearing, tobacco-juice-spitting Hank Peters hasn't worn off, and my niggling list of injuries seems a small price to pay for glory. As I'm nursing my drink and my memories, the bartender, a brunette in her late twenties, pauses in front of me.

"Want to see something hilarious?" she asks.

"Sure."

"Then check out these two clowns."

I peer up gingerly (my neck) and see a man who looks a lot like me flying at a man with a lei around his neck. Then the two flail at each other in a highly undignified manner. When they cut back to the anchor, there's a reference to a security camera at a Honolulu bar.

"How often have they been showing this?"

"A lot. Apparently, they're both professional golfers... on the *Senior* Tour."

I'm resisting the urge to ask her which of these two clowns, in her estimation, won the fight, when a call comes in on my cell from Ponte Vedra, Florida.

"Is this Travis McKinley?"

"Yes."

"This is Tim Finchem." The commissioner of the PGA tour. "I need to see you in my office tomorrow afternoon."

15

THE NEXT AFTERNOON, PETERS and I are side by side again. Instead of being perched on bar stools, our butts are nearly scraping the broadloom in a pair of low-slung leather chairs. The chairs are facing PGA Commissioner Timothy W. Finchem, who looks down at us, in every sense, from behind his brilliantly polished mahogany desk. Despite the quality of Finchem's furniture, suit, and haircut, the scene reeks of high school, specifically that doomsday moment when you're summoned to the principal's office.

For a couple of minutes, Finchem lets us twist in the over-air-conditioned breeze. As we endure the silent treatment, I notice that Peters is as banged up as me, with a badly swollen lower lip and a shiner of his own. I'm struck by how young Finchem looks. On paper, Peters and I may only have him by about five years, but he has spent a lot less time in the sun and a lot more in the gym, and it shows.

Then again, we work for a living. Kind of.

I'm also puzzled by the three black plastic cassettes on his desk. Presumably they contain the surveillance footage ESPN has been wearing out on *SportsCenter,* but why three? Has Finchem made duplicates so we can each take one home and study it before we write our essays on how we will never get caught fighting on camera in a dive bar again?

Finchem takes the top one off the stack and feeds it into the VCR, which along with a monitor has been wheeled into his office. By now I've seen the footage half a dozen times, but it doesn't get any easier. This version, which picks up the action about a minute sooner, is even more damning than the one they've been airing. A camera mounted on the far wall shows Earl and me bent over our drinks as Peters and his friends take the empty spots beside us, then captures our awkward surprise as we discover we're sitting next to each other. Finchem winces at the monitor, as if the seedy interior of the Ding Dong is desecrating his immaculate office, and seems baffled that anyone, let alone three members of the Senior Tour, would choose to be there.

For the next thirty seconds or so, the tape shows Peters attempting to engage me in conversation. While Peters's posture is upright, expansive, and friendly, I look down at the surface of the bar. Then, without any apparent provocation, I spring from my stool and attack him.

"This is from last night," says Finchem as he ejects and replaces the tape.

The screen fills with color bars, which give way to a stage on which Jay Leno is in the midst of his *Tonight Show* monologue.

"I guess you've all heard about those two palookas McKinley and Peters? Did you know HBO's doing a rematch—McKinley and Peters II? It's going to be on pay-per-view for nineteen ninety-five. Sounded pricey to me, too. Then I realized they're going to *pay us* to watch."

As Peters mimes a burlesque drummer providing a rimshot, Finchem switches cassettes again, so we can see what Letterman can do with the same material.

"You know where this fight took place?" asks Letterman, fingering a button on his double-breasted blazer. "A very classy watering hole by the name of the Ding Dong Lounge. I'm not making that up," he says, then slowly repeats the name with exaggerated clarity—"the... Ding...Dong...Lounge. I know what you're thinking— what kind of person goes to a place called the Ding Dong Lounge? Well, now we know the answer: ding-dongs. The Ding Dong Lounge is a place where ding-dongs feel welcome and at home." As the CBS Orchestra plays the theme from *Cheers,* Finchem hits Eject and the audio-video presentation is over.

"Commissioner," says Peters, "I have nothing to say about these last two tapes, except that they remind me how much I miss Carson. As for the first, it couldn't be more misleading. Based on that tape, you, or anyone else, would think Travis started this. In fact, this fight was instigated entirely by me and my big mouth. Without sound, you can't hear me taunting Travis repeatedly about what happened a few hours before in sudden death.

"Commissioner, I didn't say one or two things. I said about five, all unnecessary, all uncalled-for, and at least one came after he politely asked me to stop. Under the circumstances, I think Travis showed a lot of restraint."

"You call that restraint?"

"That's what I said, Commissioner. Restraint."

"Hank, I appreciate you standing up for your fellow competitor, but the video shows what it shows. You two have embarrassed the tour and tarnished our brand. You think the banks and investment advisors who sponsor our events want to see two of our most popular players brawling in a dive? Hank, you're on probation for the rest of the year. Travis, you're suspended for six months."

"That's ridiculous," says Peters. "If anyone should be suspended, it should be me."

But this isn't a hearing, and Finchem is already out of his chair.

"I feel terrible about this," says Peters when the two of us are alone. "And you were playing great golf. That shot on eighteen was the best shot I've seen this year. You need to borrow some money to tide you over, don't hesitate to ask. It's the least I can do."

"Thanks, Hank, I'm okay on that score. And I appreciate what you said."

"It's all true. Not that it did any good. But what do you expect from a guy who went to college on a debating scholarship? And one other thing…my friends call me Stump."

16

BEYOND THE UNFAMILIAR WINDSHIELD is an empty parking lot illuminated by the last few minutes of daylight. On the passenger seat are a half-eaten turkey sandwich and an empty can of iced tea, and I have no memory of either. The insignia on the steering wheel indicates the car is a Chrysler, and a glance over my shoulder reveals the interior of a minivan. The odometer shows 169 miles, so that explains the new-car smell, but not much else, and the clock, when I finally find it, reads 6:09. It's not until I open the glove compartment and unfold the rental agreement from the Jacksonville Airport Alamo that I remember where I am and why, and realize I've been sitting like this in the deepening dusk for nearly an hour.

For the second time in little more than a year, I've lost my job, but this one I loved and was actually quite good at. Against lotto-like odds, I achieved a lifelong quest to play competitive golf for a living, and in forty-five video-taped seconds screwed it up. A spot on the Senior Tour is fleeting to begin with. Under the best circumstances, three or four years is a pretty good run, so losing six months of my middle-aged prime is a pretty stiff price to pay for a relatively harmless fight.

Yet as stunned as I am by Finchem's harsh penalty, I'm more undone by Peters's generosity. How could I have been so wrong about the guy? I spent thirty years hating a person who didn't exist. Pressed to come up with an explanation for my dislike, I would have cited his good ol' boy routine and his redneck shtick, but I can see that was nothing but a smokeless smoke screen.

The reason I didn't like Hank Peters is because he is a better golfer than I am. And he knows it. That's not the abridged edition. It's the entire volume. You want to earn my lifelong enmity, just be better than me at something I care about, exude a little more self-confidence, and beat me in a college match in which I have you down two with three to play.

Do that, and I'll hate you for life. I promise. And how does Peters respond to all my petty bile and cranky bullshit? How does he repay me for three decades of tight-lipped, phony smiles and bad-vibing? By treating me like a friend.

According to the dashboard clock, another twenty

minutes have gone missing as mysteriously as that half a sandwich. If I'm going to make my flight, I need to hustle. I find the keys, start the car, and turn on the lights, and as I reach back for the seat belt, I catch a glimpse of the one person I least want to see.

17

My reception in Winnetka is more in keeping with the return of a conquering hero than a disgraced asshole. As I step through the front door, all three remaining full-time residents of the McKinley household—woman, child, and dog—hurl themselves at me with delight. Sarah plants a fat, juicy kiss on my mouth, Louie paws my legs and crows like a rooster, and in between, Noah wraps his arms around me and says, "Dad, that fight was awesome."

"A brawl?...In a dive bar?...With a guy named Stump?" whispers Sarah breathily in my ear. "I had no idea you were such a badass."

"Really?"

"Yeah, really."

Although it's almost midnight, I'm hustled from the foyer into the kitchen and seated at the head of the table. Noah hands me a glass of the best red on the premises, and Sarah takes a warm plate from the oven. Artfully arranged on top of it are the best parts of a roasted chicken, surrounded by potatoes simmered in its juices, and ringed by blackened Brussels sprouts.

"I made you your death row meal," says Sarah, and I try not to wince at the unintended irony.

"Everything is absurdly delicious. I only wish I deserved it."

"We think you do," says Noah, pouring himself a bowl of Cheerios.

"You've won tournaments before, Travis. This was different."

"Not in a good way. It turns out I couldn't have been more wrong about Peters."

"You've always disliked him."

"For no good reason. In our meeting with Finchem, he defended me like Clarence Darrow. Insisted the whole thing was his fault."

"Maybe it was."

"And I assume you haven't forgotten the part about me being suspended for six months."

"That's unfortunate and unfair. But you'll come back stronger than ever. We're sure of it."

"You too, pal?"

"No question," says Noah, milk trickling down his chin. Interjecting reality into this late-night celebration makes me feel like the killjoy I am. Instead, I hoist my Pinot and toast the room. "What a meal! What a wife! What a kid! What a dog!"

"That's more like it," says Sarah.

"By the way," says Noah, "did I tell you that even Mr. Wilmot in gym is treating me better?"

"Big surprise there."

After dinner, Noah trudges to bed and Sarah refuses to be talked out of washing the dishes, so I head to the couch with Louie. When he rests his head on my thigh, farts, sighs, and falls asleep, I'm grateful that at least one member of the household isn't burdened with false illusions.

18

THE NEXT MORNING, I drop Noah at school, and Louie and I take a drive to the Creekview Country Club, which is as deserted as it should be on a Wednesday morning in mid-January. I park in the rear corner, and the two of us set out up the first fairway, following the cart tracks left from my grandfather's funeral. Three weeks later, the ground is still frozen, but the temperature has soared into the high twenties, and the air is heavy with forecast snow.

On the first green, Louie and I find the spot where the first installment of my grandfather's ashes were scattered, my fallible memory confirmed by Louie's infallible nose. Whenever things get shaky, and sooner or later they always do, my first instinct is to go talk to Pop. It's been that way since I learned to walk, let alone swing a 7-iron, and it's not going to change now just because he's dead. Gazing down at the green, I fill him in on what happened in

Hawaii, from the last hole of regulation to the only hole of sudden death. Then I get him up to speed on my visit to the Ding Dong and Finchem's office before Louie and I move on.

Over the years I've gotten almost as much comfort from this old golf course as I have from my grandfather. It's not only where I learned to play, it's where over the course of thousands of rounds, I literally grew up. Or tried to. Even here, however, I can't escape the harsh glare of self-scrutiny, set off by Peters's unexpected support. As Louie and I wander in the cold from hole to hole, I rewind as much of my first fifty-one years or so as I can stomach, searching for an occasion, or preferably more, when I behaved as generously.

Ten holes later, I haven't come up with one. There is, however, no shortage of cringeworthy moments, incidents so damning I'm not going to share them now. Whenever I think I've unearthed something I can hold up in my defense—"Your Honor, I refer you to exhibit one A"—I soon see through it for what it was, a transparent attempt to impress a girl, or a friend or a college admissions staff. As far as I can tell, my only genuine acts of kindness have been directed at Sarah, Elizabeth, Simon, and Noah, and they're simply an extension of myself and inadmissible as evidence.

Being back on home turf isn't doing much for me, but

Louie is having a blast. I know every blade of grass on these suburban sixty acres, but for Louie it's all thrillingly new, and he is beside himself at having the run of such a vast, fascinating tract. Like a canine Columbus wading ashore in the New World, he races from tree to bush to rock, raising a leg and planting the flag of Louie.

On the 14th fairway, Louie picks up the scent of Simon and, barking maniacally, follows it to the portion of the green where my older son tipped Pop's ashes. What, I wonder, did my grandfather see in me? If I were nothing more than a little sawed-off bag of shit, even he wouldn't have loved me. Since he did, he must have detected a crumb of decency. Right? Or was it all just biology, a kindhearted old coot giving his flesh and blood the benefit of the doubt? Unfortunately, that sounds more like it.

As we hover over the fresh memory of Pop's remains, Louie starts barking again, this time skyward, and when I tilt my head back, it looks as if an enormous old pillow has burst open. Like Louie last night on the couch, the sky is letting it all go. Still barking, Louie sprints out into the pouring snow, and after one last aside to Pop, I head after him.

19

IT SNOWS FOR TWENTY-FOUR hours, and when I look out the window Thursday morning, Winnetka has rarely looked better. All the tacky details and worst pretensions of suburban architecture have been whited out. What's left is the snow-topped geometry of rooftops and telephone lines and the poetry of trees.

Just as lovely is the muffled quiet, and so in its own way the rattling and scraping of the first wave of municipal plows. Then the local citizenry wheel out and rev up their snow-moving toys. To escape the din, I grab my golf bag from the garage and haul it to the basement.

Downstairs, I pull out all the clubs and lean them against the wall of my workshop. It's been almost a week since I've touched my sticks, and I miss them. What happened in Hawaii wasn't their fault. At least, not entirely. Arrayed by height, from my homely Big Bertha to my lovely ancient bull's-eye, they look like the multiple generations of a large, eccentric family gathered for a portrait.

I'd clean the clubs, but Johnny A took care of that before we packed up, and the shaft, grip, lie, and loft of every one have already been tweaked and fitted to within an inch of their lives. I consider adding a couple of degrees of loft to my 4-iron to close the gap between it and my 5-wood, but decide instead to replace the grips on my wedges, which is equally unnecessary but at least not destructive. I've got my gap wedge in the vise and the old grip half off when Louie starts imitating a watchdog.

Upstairs, I open the front door to a tall, pudgy teenager, about seventeen, whose face is scarred with acne. He holds a shovel and, despite the cold, wears only a sweater, scarf, and hat, all three of which are made of the same coarse green wool and are far too sturdy and singular to have been purchased at the local mall.

"Sorry to interrupt your pliering," says the boy, referring to the pliers in my right hand. "I was hoping I could shovel your walks and driveway."

"I'd appreciate that."

"Does twenty dollars seem fair?"

"Not to you," I say. "There's at least two feet of snow, and it's wet and heavy."

"Your points are all well taken," responds the boy with

a goofy grin that outshines his acne, and his European accent underlines the arcane diction.

"Let's make it forty dollars."

"Excellent," says the kid, extending a large hand reddened by the cold. "We have a verbal contract and a handshake agreement."

Then he turns his back and starts shoveling, and while he digs his way from the front door to the driveway, I return to my subterranean busy work. In total, I manage to kill almost an hour. I replace the grips on all three wedges (twenty-five minutes), polish and clean my big white Mizuno bag (twenty minutes), then do the same to my golf shoes (ten minutes).

When I climb out of the basement, the sun is blinding and the smell of hot chocolate wafts from the kitchen. Outside, the kid has finished the walk and is attacking the driveway, and as I watch from the living room, Noah, with Louie trailing, emerges from the side of the house bearing two steaming mugs. After the shoveler accepts his, the pair chink cups and sip their warm drinks in the winter sun, chatting like old pals. Then the boy hands back the empty, makes a courtly bow, and returns to work.

"I like Jerzy," says Noah, back in the kitchen. "He's good people."

"I like him, too."

Jerzy shovels for three hours. When he returns to the front door, he holds the plastic bag containing a day-old paper. "An artifact excavated from the base of the driveway," he says. "Perhaps it will be of some interest." More conspicuous than his accent is his delight in his new language, as if every word and figure of speech is inherently amusing.

"Thanks, Jerzy. You did a hell of a job. I'm Travis."

"I know who you are, Mr. McKinley. You're Winnetka's most notorious professional athlete."

"I guess you heard about the suspension."

"It struck me as rather draconian."

"Ditto. You play?" I ask.

"Unfortunately not, but I spectate via television."

I pull two twenties and a ten from my wallet and, as I hand them over, notice that the acne on his forehead camouflages a nasty gash.

"This is too much," says Jerzy.

"Not at all. You earned it. What happened to your head?"

"Tripped on the ice. Unfortunately, both my feet are left ones."

"Well, good luck getting back. And thanks again."

20

I RIP THROUGH THE wet wrapper, and without so much as a glance at the world, local, business, and cultural news, apply myself directly to Sports. An unseemly amount of the first page is devoted to the exploits of Michael Jordan, who led the Bulls to victory last night in Texas, and there's a photo of him throwing one down over San Antonio's rookie center, Tim Duncan.

I'll get back to that in a moment, but first I want to see how Earl is faring in Tampa. Among the box scores and standings, I find the leaderboard for the GTE Suncoast Classic, where order has been restored. Tied for the lead are Hale Irwin and Gil Morgan, and four strokes back is Earl Fielder. It looks like Earl is going to have to wait another week before getting that first *w*, but back-to-back 69s are nothing to sneeze at and almost certain to lead to his twenty-fifth top ten in a row. There's no sign of

Stump. Most likely, he took the week off to enjoy his victory and give his face a chance to look more presentable.

I sip my coffee and study the small type like a tax attorney searching for loopholes. From the box score, I learn that Jordan scored thirty-five points in thirty-three minutes, shooting eight for fifteen from the field, four for nine from three-point range, and seven for seven from the line, and Pippen was one assist and two rebounds short of a triple-double. My scrutiny shifts from the NBA standings to the Blackhawks box score to the college basketball results (Eastern Michigan 68, Northwestern 52) before alighting on "Transactions." If the agate are the crumbs of the sports section, then "Transactions" are the crumbs of the crumbs. But where else would I learn that the Bears have agreed to a four-year contract with outside linebacker Boswell King and waived (football is even crueler than golf) defensive lineman Simon Briggs and placed Ted Keating on injured reserve? Or that Phil Jackson has been fined $10,000 for criticizing the officials after last week's loss in Portland, which strikes me as rather draconian?

What, you may wonder, is so interesting about an endless succession of contrived contests staged day after day, night after night, in gyms, rinks, and arenas? For one thing, they're easy to digest. Someone won. Someone lost. Someone, like yours truly, screwed up, and someone, like Hank Peters, didn't. The rest of the paper is never that clear, and even if you learn what happened, you don't know what it means. Maybe you'll know in a week or a month. More likely, you never will.

I spend over an hour of the only life I'll ever have poring over scores, standings, and minutiae, and just when I think I've extracted every last bit of infotainment from these four pages of newsprint, I stumble on half a dozen paragraph-sized morsels herded under "Briefs." The headline for the golf item reads: CADDIES INJURED IN CRASH.

Two regular caddies on the Senior Tour were injured yesterday afternoon on Route 75 ten miles outside of Tampa, Florida, when their van swerved to avoid a deer. GW Cable of Sarasota, Florida, was treated for a concussion and held overnight and Brandon Fielder of Monroe, North Carolina, was treated for a broken arm and released.

The news that Earl is without a caddy jolts me upright. Suddenly restless, I get up and wash out the saucepan Noah used to make the hot chocolate and place it in the drying rack. Outside the kitchen window a black squirrel clings to the top of the bird feeder. Hanging upside down, he struggles to extract a couple of seeds, an athletic challenge with more at stake than any of those I read about.

As the bird feeder swings back and forth, I recall the fateful day when Earl and I were paired in the second round of Q-School, and how my immediate comfort with him helped me through the round. Then I think of our even more important meeting four days later, after I squeaked through and he fell just short, when he volunteered to carry my bag for my rookie season.

If the situation had been reversed, and he had gotten through and I had narrowly missed out, would I have even considered making him the same offer? I know the answer, but why not? Earl is single, with a pension and an impressive stock portfolio, so I would have needed a job more than him. Is it because I'm a snob who considers caddying beneath him? And is part of that snobbism based on race? More likely, it's because I would have been sulking too much to think objectively.

What I would or might have done years ago is interesting, at least to me. The more pressing question is what am I going to do now? Before I have a chance to chicken out, I grab the phone and call Earl.

21

THREE DAYS LATER, WEARING a white bib with FIELDER pinned to the back, I'm standing like a statue behind the first tee of the Longboat Key Club & Resort, site of the Greater Sarasota Intellinet Challenge. Although my only immediate responsibility is to make sure Earl's bag doesn't topple over in the middle of his backswing, I'm more nervous than if I were the one teeing it up, and as Earl takes his practice swings, I thumb the corner of the index card in my back pocket like a security blanket.

Due to the blizzard, I couldn't get a flight out of Chicago till this morning and didn't screech into the parking lot till forty minutes ago. That was barely enough time to fill out that index card with the distances Earl hits all his clubs and grab a yardage book, and as Earl settles behind the ball, I tap them both again to make sure they're still there. Then Earl pipes his drive down the center, and I hoist his bag over my right shoulder and hustle after him.

The lack of time to prepare certainly contributes to my agitation. A bigger factor is Earl's reaction when I volunteered my services. Let's just say he didn't jump at the offer. After ten seconds of awkward silence, the best he could come up with was "You sure you want to do this? The bag's pretty heavy."

"I know," I said. "I just carried mine down to the basement."

"Imagine what it will feel like after six miles."

"You didn't have any trouble."

"Yeah. Well, I'm not you."

That night at dinner, Sarah and Noah were just as skeptical about my suitability for hard anonymous labor. An informal poll of best friend and family yielded the unflattering consensus that I was too much of a pussy and too much of a prima donna to happily hump a forty-pound bag with another man's name on it.

I don't say a word as I escort Earl down a tight fairway lined with modest houses and screened-in swimming pools. Pacing off yardages, pulling clubs, and reading greens will be enough of a challenge without engaging in small talk, and I want to make it clear from the outset that I'm not here to hang out but to work.

Despite my determination to exceed everyone's low expectations, I narrowly avoid disaster, and it happens on the very first hole, after Earl follows his perfect drive with a crisp 7-iron that leaves him twenty-two feet below the hole. One of the great perks of being a professional golfer, right up there with not having to work for a living, is that eighteen times a round, you get to flaunt your good fortune by performing a simple ritual permissible only for pros—the mark and toss. Upon finding your ball on the green, you saunter up behind it, mark the spot, then toss the ball to your caddy, who wipes it clean with a damp towel.

Every pro performs this little sequence in his own inimitable fashion, but always with as much nonchalance as he can muster with a straight face. Some players release the ball without even a glance at their caddy, like a look-away pass in basketball. Others lob it like a baby hook. Earl's signature is to put a bit of air under it, and when he flips it to me, perhaps as a joke or perhaps as a kind of initiation, he puts even more than usual, and the height of the toss gives me way too much time to consider the consequences of booting it.

Mainly, I'm thinking about the pond, directly behind me at the base of a closely mown slope, and the fact that the surface is coated with opaque green slime. If I yip the catch, not only will Earl's ball end up in the soup, but there'll be no way to find it, and based on my rereading on the flight down of that page-turner known as *The Rules of Golf*, I know that if Earl has to putt out with a different ball than the one he just threw to me, I'll go down in looping lore as the rookie who cost his player two strokes on his first hole. As a result, I brace myself for this little pop-up as if it were a vicious line drive and, with two hands extended and Earl's clubs bouncing around on my back, am barely able to corral it.

"Nice catch," says Earl.

Six holes later, I find another way to amuse my new boss. Because it's a muggy Florida afternoon, I'm careful to stay hydrated, so careful I'm soon in need of a bathroom. I put it off as long as a man of a certain age can, but when there's a wait at the par-three 7th, I jump at the chance and scurry to the small white stucco structure discreetly tucked among a cluster of shading palms. Unfortunately, a tournament official got there first and tacked a sign to the door: FOR PLAYERS ONLY.

That leaves the plastic Porta-Potty roasting in the sun ten yards away. "Enjoy the facilities?" asks Earl when I get back.

"Immensely. Thanks for asking."

22

Earl shoots 71 in the first round and 71 in the second. Then again, Earl's rounds often mirror each other. That's why he's the Joe DiMaggio of senior golf, with twenty-four consecutive top tens and counting. The man doesn't make bad swings or hit squirrelly shots.

Earl's got one of the most repeatable swings on the planet. I've always known this, of course, but witnessing it up close and personal is a little disconcerting. Again and again, I pace off the distance to the nearest sprinkler head, do the math, and come up with the same number to the center of the green on Saturday that we had on Friday. Once, I'm quite certain, his ball came to rest on top of his old filled-in divot.

For his caddy, it's as frustrating as it is impressive, because despite his otherworldly ball-striking, we're a whopping two under. He doesn't make bogeys, but he doesn't make birdies, either. He's the human unhigh-light film.

So where does Earl drag me after the second round is in the books? The driving range, of course. Like everyone else, Earl likes to practice what he's good at. It reminds me of the greasers in high school who would spend all afternoon waxing and polishing their already gleaming Camaros and GTOs.

"You know how many fairways you missed the first two days?" I ask, after I've seen one too many perfect 5-irons.

"Not a lot."

"One. By six inches. You also missed twenty-four putts inside twenty feet. And guess how many you got to the hole?"

"Not enough."

"Two."

"Wow, Travis. You're actually paying attention."

"That stuff you said about how you would trade all those thirds and fourths for one win. Was that bullshit?"

"No."

"Then put that club away and follow me."

To my relief, he does, and we spend the next three hours on the practice green performing one drill. From anywhere from eight to sixty feet, I drop six balls, and he has to get every one to the hole. If he doesn't, we start over.

Want to know the results of this three-hour master

class? I was afraid you might. On Sunday, Earl doesn't make a putt over six feet and leaves just as many short. Thanks to my meddling, he shoots 72 and finishes out of the top ten for the first time in a year. I violated the caddy's version of the Hippocratic oath, which is not to make things worse. And yet, as I throw my bag in the trunk and motor south, I'm buoyed by an almost giddy sense of optimism.

23

THE REASON I'M SO hopeful is that our next stop, Shoal Creek, just outside Birmingham, Alabama, is the toughest track the seniors play all year. That means Earl, even with me on the bag, has a real chance. Let me explain.

Most of the tournaments out here, like the one we just wrapped up in Sarasota, are held at resorts. Resort courses play easy. They have to, because they're laid out with the hacker in mind. The fairways are wide, the rough anemic, and the hazards so close to the tee they're not really in play, at least not for the pros, who start drooling all over themselves before they get out of their cars. Since keeping the ball in play isn't much of a challenge, these tournaments turn into putting contests, and Earl isn't going to win many of those.

At Shoal Creek, which was carved out of the woods by Nicklaus in '77 and has already hosted two PGA championships, no one's salivating in the parking lot. It's long and tight and unforgiving and there are no houses and swimming pools lining the fairways. To contend at Shoal Creek, you need to be a bona fide ball-striker, someone who can drive it long *and* straight and hit greens from 200 yards out all day. Even on the Senior Tour, there aren't many of these, and Earl is one of them. Once you get to the deep end of his bag, he's as good as any old fart in the world.

In Birmingham, Earl and I have three days to prepare, and the more we see of the course, the worse it looks and the more I like it. Not only is the course hard, it's set up hard too, with four inches of the juiciest Bermuda rough this side of a U.S. Open. In our first practice round, I drop three balls into it and invite Earl, one of the stronger guys out here, to hack away with his 7-iron. His best carries 85 yards.

"This stuff is horrible," says Earl.

"No, it's not. It's beautiful. Because you're not going to be in it. And a lot of your so-called friends will be."

24

My biggest fear is that Earl wants it too much. Ever since we rolled into town the press has been all over both of us. A former U.S. Senior Open winner who gets himself suspended, then comes out to caddy for his old pal, is good copy, and part of what makes it intriguing, particularly in Alabama, is that the golfer is black and the caddy white. When Shoal Creek hosted their first PGA Championship in 1984, which, by the way, was won by Trevino, the club's all-white membership became a national story after Hall Thompson, its founder and president, defended his club by saying "we don't discriminate in every other area except blacks." Since then, Thompson has changed his tune, at least slightly, and added one African-American to the roster, but a black golfer winning the tournament would still be newsworthy, maybe even historic.

In the press tent, Earl insists he couldn't care less about any of that. "Winning my first tournament is all the incentive I need," he says. That's true, as far as it goes, but the racial backstory gives him all the more incentive. Why wouldn't it? And you can tell that it means something to the club's black caddies, who go out of their way to shake his hand, wish him luck, or just make eye contact.

If Earl won't talk about it, maybe I will. In the last three days, I've received dozens of interview requests, including one from ESPN's Stuart Scott, who suggests I might want to be known for something other than the Ding Dong Lounge. I turn them all down—the last thing I want to do is say something stupid that will put extra pressure on Earl—and Thursday night, when there's a knock on my hotel door, I ignore it like all the rest.

After thirty seconds, it turns into banging.

"Travis, open up. I know you're in there."

Annoyed, I hop from the bed and unchain the door. It's Stump.

"I want to wish you good luck," he says. "I think it's great that you're out here with Earl."

"Thanks, Stump. I hope Earl feels the same."

"Believe it or not, he does. I just ran into the Duke of Earl in the elevator. He told me you actually know what you're doing. Surprised the hell out of him."

"I bet. Speaking of surprises, thanks again for what you

said in Ponte Vedra. It really opened my eyes. For thirty years I didn't like you very much."

"I kind of deduced that."

"All because you beat me in a college match thirty fucking years ago."

"You mean the one where you had me down by two with three to go?" says Stump with a shit-eating grin.

"Yeah, that one."

"You're a competitive prick, Travis. So am I and so is Earl and every other asshole out here. We wouldn't be here otherwise. If it makes you feel any better, I always thought you were an asshole, too."

"But you were right."

"Yeah, good point."

Then Stump leans forward and points at a spot above my collar, like he can't quite believe what he's seeing. "No doubt about it," he says. "That's raw and pink and angry. It's official, son. You're a redneck now, too."

25

THE FINAL PIECE OF bad/good news is the weather. On Monday, the temperature barely reached sixty, and it has gotten colder and windier ever since. This morning, when we finally tee off for real, it's forty-eight, with twenty-five-mile-an-hour gusts. On this course with this setup and this wind, it's about survival, and who knows more about that than someone who got himself home in one piece from four tours in Vietnam?

For the next four and a half hours, Earl and I keep our heads down and plot our way from point A to B to C, following the routes we mapped out for each hole. Off the tee, Earl keeps it out of the wind with a low, hard stinger even Tiger wouldn't sneeze at. Although the ball doesn't get more than twenty feet off the ground, he gets so much roll that he puts it out there 275/280 every time, and while Earl's playing partners, one of whom is the golf commentator and Senior Tour rookie Gary McCord, are hacking it out of the rough every three or four holes, Earl doesn't stray from the short grass.

I'm not saying Earl makes it look easy. The human un-highlight film isn't endowed with that kind of flair. But he makes it look boring, which is even better, as far as I'm concerned. Fairway, green, two putts. Fairway, green, two putts. After six holes of this, I overhear McCord mumble to his caddy, "I think that motherfucker is an android."

Earl's got things so under control, I can enjoy the rugged scenery. When I say Shoal Creek was carved out of the woods, I mean real woods, and unlike most courses we play, the wilderness hasn't been utterly obliterated so a bunch of middle-aged guys can play golf. There have been sightings of foxes, coyotes, and bears, and except for a brick chimney high on Double Oak Mountain, which looks down over the 14th hole, the views aren't marred by houses.

The first round is classic Earl—fourteen of fourteen fairways, fifteen greens in regulation, and thirty-four putts. One birdie, one bogey, and sixteen pars. That's just fine, because for once, he's playing a course where par means something. Earl's opening 72 leaves him tied for third, two strokes out of the lead.

26

Saturday's just as raw and gusty, and now it's raining. By the third hole, it's coming down hard and we all expect play to be suspended, but with no electricity on the radar, the marshals decide to have us slog on. The wet fairways make the course longer and harder, which plays into Earl's strengths, but I'm more than a little worried about holding up my end of the bargain, since the one thing harder than playing golf in the wind and the cold is caddying in the rain.

Add a downpour to the equation and caddying becomes borderline impossible. Ever try carrying the bag, cleaning and pulling clubs, pacing off yardages, and deciphering the wind and greens while holding an umbrella over your golfer? It's like being a short-order cook at a popular diner on a busy morning, when you've got a grill full of crackling eggs and new orders piling up. There's too much to do, and if you crumble under the pressure, you're toast, as in whiskey down. To keep Earl and his equipment dry, I've got four towels in rotation—two in the bag, one under my jacket, and one hanging from the tines of Earl's umbrella beside an extra glove—and all I'm trying to do is stay calm so Earl can stay calm, too.

"Bearing up okay?" asks Earl as I swap a soaking towel for a semidry one.

"Piece of cake," I lie. "You just concentrate on fairways and greens."

Earl does as instructed. He's like the U.S. Postal Service. Neither wind nor cold nor rain can stop him from delivering pars. On the par-five 10th, he even throws in a birdie, and when the horn blows to stop play with Earl safely on the 12th green, I'm disappointed, because I doubt anyone else is faring as well under these conditions.

Till now, I've been too busy to verify that, but as Earl and I thread our way back to the clubhouse, we get our first look at the leaderboard. At the very top, so high it hurts my neck, is the name on the back of my overalls—Earl Fielder—and beside it the only number in red, –1, because he's the only golfer under par.

"Take a gander at that," I say.

"Let's not get too worked up yet. We haven't even played thirty holes. Speaking of which, as soon as we're done here, you should head back to the hotel and take it easy. Tomorrow's going to be a marathon."

27

I carry Earl's dripping bag through the hotel lobby and into the elevator, and when I get off on the third floor, there's a puddle in the corner. Inside my room, I pull all the clubs and dry the grips with a bath towel. Then I crank the tin heater to 11, lay the soaking bag in front of it, and head back out the door.

When I drive back through the stone pillars, Shoal Creek is empty. After a day like today the players can't get away fast enough, and the only people milling about the grounds are the employees of the beverage companies, who are here to restock the hospitality tents for Sunday. In its soggy way, the course is as lovely in the damp gloaming as in blazing sunshine, and as I walk past the abandoned clubhouse, I can hear the water running down the gutters and dripping off the leaves.

Beyond the clubhouse is the pro shop, the retail outlet

tastefully tucked away in a Colonial-style house with an eagle over the front door, and tacked to the rear of it like an afterthought is the low-slung caddy shack. Since the touring pros brought their own and the course is closed to members, there's no work for the regular caddies this week. Nevertheless, a handful have come in to help each other while away a miserable day. Three play dominoes, a solitary tall figure stretches out over a pool table, and a fifth stands between them stuffing kindling into a pot-belly stove that glows orange at the center of the room. The man stoking the fire seems the most approachable.

"That little stove throws off some heat," I offer.

"Better than nothing."

"I'm Travis. I'm caddying for one of the seniors this week."

"Lucky you."

"It's going to take more than luck to win tomorrow. That's why I'm here."

"Who's got you on the bag?"

"Earl Fielder."

"Why didn't you say so?" says the man, unlocking a smile and extending his hand. "I'm Vince. How can I help you?"

"I'm looking to talk to someone who knows a lot more about this track than me. Hopefully, someone willing to share what he knows."

"I wouldn't be of much use. As the caddy master, I'm only on the course on Mondays, when they let us play. Those three aren't what you're looking for either. They're what we call bag toters. The person you need to talk to is Ron Bouler," he says, pointing toward the pool table. "Owl's been looping here since the day it opened. He knows every blade of grass on this plantation. I'll introduce you.

"Hey, Owl," says Vince, "someone's here to pick your brain." Bouler, who wears a leather cap, is setting up to bank the six ball in the far corner, and when he swivels his head toward me, I see why he was nicknamed after a bird of prey.

"Travis is caddying for Earl Fielder this week and is looking for an edge, things you can't find in the yardage book." Without taking his eyes from me, Bouler slides his stick forward. The chipped cue hits the evergreen ball dead center, sending it caroming the full length of the table into the corner pocket.

"Travis," says Bouler, "aren't you the one who got into it in Hawaii?"

"'Fraid so."

"And now you're caddying for a brother. How the mighty have fallen."

"I'm just trying to return a favor and help a friend get his first win. Tomorrow, I want every advantage I can get."

"Local knowledge."

"Exactly. As much as you can spare and I can absorb in one night. I want to know how the greens will handle all this water. Which putts are going to look faster than they are and which are going to be slower? Which ones are going to break half an inch less than they look like they will and which ones will break half an inch more? What are the worst patches on every green and fairway? Where are you as good as dead and what can you live with?"

"You bring the chart of where they're cutting the holes tomorrow?" As he puts down his cue, I pull a damp piece of paper from my rain jacket, unfold it, and hand it to him. When Bouler leans into the light, I'm surprised by how young he is, midthirties tops.

"I stopped going to school after ninth grade," says Bouler as he studies Sunday's pin positions. "You were wondering how I could have caddied here since seventy-seven. Well, that's how."

"Math was never my strong point," I say.

"It was mine, but I couldn't afford to stay in school. Not if I wanted to eat, too. I started here at fifteen, actually before that. I grew up a mile down the road. When they brought in the big earthmoving machines to lay out the course, I rode over on my bike and watched. I saw the greens when they were just mounds of dirt, and when it poured like today, I watched the way the water ran over them. That's the way the putts still roll."

Owl turns his eyes from me and calls back to Vince, who's reading at the desk near the front door. "Vince, any chance you could put on another pot of coffee? Travis and me, we got some homework to do."

28

By Sunday morning, the rain has cleared. It feels more like early September than late February, and that first-day-of-school edge in the air does nothing to ease my tension. Earl's feeling it, too. On the range early, just after dawn, he hits a couple of balls off-center.

For those who didn't complete yesterday's round, there's a shotgun start at 8:16 a.m., and shortly before that our threesome is ferried out to the dew-covered 12th green, where the previous afternoon, Earl marked his ball in the rain. The 460-yard 12th is a brute of a par 4, and reaching the green in regulation was no mean feat. Still, there's a lot of work to be done. If you placed the ball by hand, you couldn't come up with a longer or more difficult putt on this green.

Earl's marker sits on the right edge, and the hole is cut on the far left. In between is a seventy-five-foot travelogue that features two knolls and a steep drop. The first half of the putt is uphill and slow and the second half is the opposite, with a dozen feet of break from right to left. After a couple of minutes to digest it, Earl shakes his head and says, "It's like putting over a camel... that's drinking water."

While Earl walks the width of the green and surveys the putt from both sides, I refer to my notes from last night's cram session at the caddy shack. Before Owl focused on the pin placements for the third round, he spent a good ten minutes breaking down this first crucial, tone-setting putt, and since I could tell him where Earl had marked his ball, he could be extremely specific. He even made a little sketch:

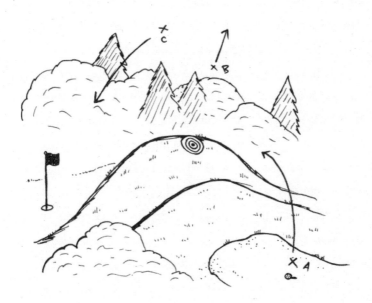

"The first key," I say, "is hitting it firm enough to get it to the top of the second knoll." I make a point of avoiding the word *hump*. "The second is getting it right enough to account for the break. Because of the rain, the first half of the putt is even slower than it seems. You need to hit it twenty percent harder than it looks. The second half of the putt will be hardly affected by the rain. The back half of the green always drains a lot better than the front."

I walk to the apex of the putt and point to a spot on the right side of the second knoll. "This is our target. If you can get the ball to die here, the slope will do the rest."

For a second Earl appraises me as coolly as the putt. Although he doesn't say a word, I know what he's thinking: *When the fuck did you become an authority on the drainage of the 12th green at Shoal Creek?*

On the practice green, I had Earl hit a dozen putts of similar length, but there was no way to prepare him for these contours or the pressure of having to deal with them on his first stroke of the day, and when he replaces the marker with the ball and squats behind it, I can see he's still struggling to believe in both himself and me.

"Earl, I did my homework. The line is perfect. You got to trust it." Earl makes three long practice strokes, takes one last peek at his distant target, and gives it a roll. The hit is solid and the ball easily crests the first knoll, slows as it climbs the second, and settles at the top, exactly what

I asked for, except that the ball has come to a complete halt. For the next couple of seconds it doesn't budge. It just sits there like Louie refusing to take a walk, and it's not clear if it's going to stay put or roll back to Earl's feet. Instead, it makes a quarter turn forward and then, after a second pause, another, until once again it is on its merry way.

When it stops for the third time, it's three inches from the hole.

"Hell of a putt, Earl."

"No, Travis, it was a hell of a read."

Compared to that, the next six holes are a piece of cake. Earl pars them all, and his 71 keeps him perched at the top of the leaderboard, two up on the only other golfers who managed to shoot par in the second round. Hale Irwin and Gil Morgan, who else?

29

"LET'S GO, EARL."

"Come on, baby."

"Time to go to work, big fellah."

Earl attracts some of the most boisterous galleries out here, particularly since he laced up his Reeboks and went back to Vietnam. Nevertheless, this crowd is louder, warmer, looser, and funkier than any that we've experienced so far.

"We at Shoal Creek or Soul Creek?" asks Earl with a smile.

"Come on, Travis," says a mellifluous southern voice I recognize as Owl's. "You got to bring it, too."

Hearing my name called out elicits a quizzical look from Earl. "Travis, you got family down here?"

"Not that I know of."

This is Earl's first time going off in the final group

on Sunday, let alone with Morgan and Irwin, and the southern hospitality is just what he needs. He comes out of the gate striping the ball with his characteristic precision and gets right back on the par train he's been riding since dawn. Unfortunately, conditions have been steadily improving since then, and by the time we approach the green of the par-five 3rd, a chilly, blustery morning has blossomed into a gorgeous Alabama afternoon without a trace of wind. The perfect weather and receptive greens are not a propitious combination, at least not for Earl, because it means that par isn't going to get it done after all, and as if to emphasize the point, Irwin rolls in a twenty-six-footer for birdie and Morgan rolls his twenty-two-footer on top of it, cutting Earl's precious lead to one.

If Earl's going to get his name engraved in silver, he's going to have to go low too, and as I learned from Earl in Sarasota and Louie in Winnetka, it's not easy teaching a middle-aged dog new tricks. On 5, Earl has an eminently makeable eighteen-footer of his own for birdie, and after referring to my crib sheet, I pass on this wisdom from Owl: two inches right and firm. Earl starts it on line but comes up half a foot short, as usual, and on the next four holes he leaves three more birdie putts in the jaws. When we walk off 9, Earl's lead is gone with the wind (and the cold and the rain) and the Birmingham chapter of Earl's Platoon is as frustrated as his caddy.

Not that Earl lets it affect his ball-striking. He opens the back nine with two more solidly struck shots to give himself yet another legitimate birdie chance. This one is from nineteen feet, not that it really matters, and as Earl looks it over, I return to Owl's notes and diagrams, sickened at the thought of all this proprietary reconnaissance coming to naught.

"Looks like an inch and a half off the right to me," says Earl. "What do you think?"

"I know exactly what it is. But why bother reading 'em if you're not going to get the ball to the goddamned hole?"

Amazed, Earl stares at me hard, and I meet him halfway. "Right edge," I say, and slap the Bridgestone in his palm.

"Jesus Christ," he says. "One forty-five-second fight and you're a certified motherfucker." Then he bangs the nineteen-footer into the back of the cup.

"You're welcome," I say.

30

WHAT FOLLOWS IS THE rarest of phenomena—an Earl Fielder birdie binge.

Earl follows up his birdie on 10 with three more on 11, 12, and 14. With that last ten-footer, he snatches back the lead at five under, one better than Morgan and two up on Irwin, and the ruckus raised by Earl's Platoon echoes off Double Oak Mountain.

Now it's just a matter of coaxing Earl back to the sprawling antebellum clubhouse, and using my proprietary database of local knowledge, I walk him through three stress-free two-putts. On 15, I get him to play a twenty-two-footer like it's thirty. On 16, I add two inches of break, and on 17, I pass along Owl's instruction to ignore what he sees and hit it straight.

As a result, Earl steps up to the 18th hole with both his lead and his nerves intact, and as he has all day, he pipes another drive straight up Broadway. I walk off the yardage to the nearest sprinkler head and do the math, then do it two more times just to be sure. As I told Owl, math was never my strong point. Three times I get the same numbers—158 yards to the middle, 143 to the hole, but with water in front, I'm only thinking about that second number, the one to the center of the green.

The prospect of delivering Earl his first PGA win has me approximately as worked up as watching Elizabeth be born, and I pull the index card from my back pocket one last time, not for the distances Earl hits all his clubs, which I've long since memorized, as much as for the tactile comfort of its softened edges. In the last two weeks that card has been in and out of that pocket and the rain so many times, it's as faint and frayed as the Shroud of Turin, but the barely legible numbers confirm what I already know—that 158 is a garden-variety 7-iron. If there's half as much adrenaline coursing through Earl as me, 7 is a little too much club and will put him in the back half of the green, but with water in front, there's no way I'm pulling less.

"It's a generic driving range seven," I say. "You're going to be a little pumped, but back of the green is just fine."

"I agree," says Earl. "Got to be the seven. I don't want to be anywhere near that water."

I pull the club and Earl goes through his brisk routine of two practice swings and a waggle. As he slides the club behind the ball, the wind, which has been nowhere to be seen or felt for two hours, picks up, and with it, just as suddenly, comes a light shower. As Earl steps away from the shot, I open the umbrella, hand it to Earl, and toss up a tuft of grass, which blows straight back into my face. After a couple of minutes of discreet stalling, I toss another pinch in the air and it comes back with interest.

"With the rain and wind I'm thinking six."

"I'm with you," says Earl. "It's got to be the six."

I put back the seven and, still holding the umbrella over his head—now the rain is coming down even harder—I hand him the 6.

"Nice and smooth. Nothing fancy."

After two practice swings and a waggle, Earl turns on the ball and hits it just as pure and solid as he does on the range 365 days a year, except in leap year, when's its 366, and it's all over the flag . . . until it splashes in the back of the pond.

With a horrible sinking feeling, I drop my eyes to Earl's bag and confirm what I already know. The 6-iron hasn't moved. It's still there. In the wind and the rain and the adrenaline, and whatever other excuses I'll come up with over the next three or four decades, I handed him the 9 instead of the 6.

After a drop, a pitch, and two putts, Earl finishes with a double bogey and adds one more top five to a resume already bursting with them.

31

FOR THE SECOND TIME in a month, Earl feels obliged to take me out and get me hammered. To dilute the misery, he invites Stump to join us, and Stump, a frequent visitor to Birmingham, insists he knows just the spot. Its official name is the Plaza, but to regulars it's the Upside Down because the sign above the door is flipped over, and as we duck beneath it and descend the stairs, I tell myself it's got to be a coincidence and not a twisted reference to the upside-down 6 that I handed Earl on 18.

To be fair, Stump might just as likely have chosen the Plaza because he likes it. As we discovered in Honolulu, the three of us share a weakness for dives, and the Upside Down is certainly a fine example, right up there—or down there—with the Ding Dong, and after grabbing our three-dollar shots and two-dollar beers, we settle into a cozy corner in the blue glow of the jukebox. Beyond the pool tables and the pinball machines is a redbrick wall festooned with graffiti, including the terse posting GET OVER IT.

Easier said than done.

To my relief, Earl is taking my screw-up better than me. In fact, he seems unfazed, and after my second shot, I can't resist the urge to verify that. "Earl, you're really not mad at me?"

"Travis, why the hell would I be mad? You busted your ass for me for two weeks, and did a hell of a job."

"With one little...I guess not so little...exception," interjects Stump.

"When you called, I thought I was doing you a favor," says Earl. "I was wrong. You lit a fire under my ass. I had four birdies on the back nine! At Shoal Creek! On a Sunday! When was the last time you saw me do that? Never. I don't go that low at my muni back home. I couldn't have done that without you."

"Or Owl," I say.

"Yeah, let's not forget Owl all of a sudden," says Stump, hoisting his mug.

"When you told me to get the fucking ball to the hole on twelve, that was beautiful. Exactly what I needed to hear. And the best part about eighteen is there's no scar tissue...because I can blame it entirely on you."

"Wonderful."

"It really is," says Earl.

"You know what we need?" says Stump, digging a couple of quarters out of his pocket. "Music." He walks to the jukebox, and before he gets back, the unmistakable sound of Hendrix's guitar pours out.

"I wouldn't have thought a redneck like you had any use for Jimi," says Earl.

"There's a lot about me you don't know, son."

"I guess so."

"For example, you probably didn't know I can sing. You're looking at the five-time karaoke champion at the Frog Tavern in Macon, Georgia."

And he can. When Hendrix starts to sing, Stump, clenching his Pabst like a mike, is right there with him, shamelessly adding extra syllables to one-vowel words, like *sun* and *shine,* in the time-honored rock star tradition.

IF THE SUHUNNNNN REFUSED TO
  SHINNNNNNNE
I DON'T MIND.

"Stump, you motherfucking bucket of shit," I say.

32

"WHAT NOW, TRAVIS?" ASKS Sarah two days later at breakfast. "Any plans?"

"Sarah, I've been out of work eight minutes, less if you consider I worked the weekend."

"I know. But we love you and want to keep you out of trouble, so we're just wondering, like I said, if you had any plans?"

"As a matter of fact, I was thinking about it on the flight back, that is when I wasn't seeing Earl's Bridgestone dive into that pond. No disrespect to Jack, but it's kind of a cliché to put water in front of the last green, don't you think?"

Sarah makes a circular motion with her index finger.

"I thought I'd spend a week practicing, then fly back down to Florida and play a couple of events on one of the mini-tours not under the auspices of the PGA. The courses are dog tracks and the prize money worse, but the best players are at least as good as the seniors, and if nothing else, it will give me an idea of what I need to work on. When I'm back, I figure I'll write a long, heartfelt letter to my pal Finchem and try to convince him that I've been rehabilitated. I'll explain that caddying for Earl and slumming on the mini-tours have given me time to take a long, hard look at myself. If he buys it, he may knock a couple of months off my suspension."

"Sounds very reasonable, Travis."

"You seem surprised."

"Not at all."

"And how about you, Noah? Does this meet with your approval?"

"Absolutely," says the kindergartner as he shovels Cheerios into his mouth.

"Good. Because those are my plans, at least my medium-range ones. Short-term, I'm taking Louie for a walk."

33

OUTSIDE, IT'S STILL SUBURBAN Chicago. Still February. Still cold as hell. Although there hasn't been another snowfall, the old snow hasn't gone anywhere, and after lying around for two weeks, it's not nearly as picturesque.

Louie, who has a coat like a woolly mammoth, is undaunted by the chill and as relieved to be out of the kitchen as me. Spewing steam from both nostrils, he struts up the block like a cop walking his beat. As he writes tickets in yellow script to potential interlopers, school buses pick up students and commuters stride purposefully to their cars, and even if it has only been eight minutes, their well-dressed haste makes me feel underemployed.

With nothing beckoning except my frigid stall at Big Oaks, I give Louie the reins and encourage him to take his sweet time. Straying beyond our usual four blocks reminds me how much the neighborhood has changed since Sarah and I moved in twenty-seven years ago. Every other house has been razed, rebuilt, or added to within an inch of its life, and the new construction is bloated and out of scale for the half-acre lots. In many cases, there's no yard left, and what's the point of paying down a mortgage if you can't walk out on a summer evening and have a catch or hit a few chips?

A block away and across the street is a turreted eyesore, and in front of it, a dozen slouching teens wait on their bus. Standing among them—but not with them—is a tall student wearing a green wool cap.

"Hey, Louie, look. It's Jerzy."

I wave but fail to get Jerzy's attention. As he gazes into the distance like an explorer scanning the horizon, three classmates in shiny black parkas saunter over. By way of greeting, the middle one punches him in the stomach. Then the other two, who are bigger, join the fun. As Louie and I look on, pinned to the wrong side of the street by brisk commuter traffic, one knocks the books from Jerzy's hands. The third kicks them down the street.

34

TRANSFORMING BIG OAKS INTO Augusta National requires not only concentration but a certain level of optimism, and after witnessing what happened to Jerzy, I'm not feeling it. Instead of dogwoods and doglegs, I see a school bus rolling down an upscale suburban street, and instead of my line and trajectory, I picture Jerzy trapped inside, doing his best to act like what just happened didn't, avoiding eye contact with his classmates as assiduously as they avoid his.

Unable to float a color-corrected daydream, I lower my sights and aim my 8-iron at the filthy Srixon banner hanging from the wire mesh at the end of the range. I had a feeling Jerzy saw me waving from across the street, and now I'm certain of it. His not wanting to acknowledge me suggests he knew what was about to happen, and that probably means it happens a lot. And so much for that explanation for the wound on his forehead.

After a dozen desultory swings, I abort my practice and walk across the street to a diner, where I nurse a coffee till it's time to pick up Noah. Reflecting on this morning leads inevitably to thoughts of Noah, who, like me, took an instant shine to Jerzy. Let's face it, Noah is a bit of an odd duck himself. Does that mean he's going to have to deal with this crap in a few years?

At Belltown Grammar, three yellow and black buses are lined up in the lot. Manufacturers must make them look antiquated on purpose. In forty years, they've barely changed. Is that why they stir such strong feelings and pop up in so many coffee commercials? This afternoon, they seem sinister in their indifference.

Lost in thought, I don't notice Noah until he opens the front door.

"How was practice, Dad? Bring Augusta to its knees?"

"Actually, I just hit balls."

"Really?"

Now he's the one worried about me.

35

THE NEXT MORNING IS worse, because like Jerzy, I know it's going to happen again.

I had hoped to reach the bus stop sooner, but Louie doesn't take well to being hustled, and by the time the turrets loom, the school bus has made the turn onto Parade Hill Road. Like yesterday, Jerzy is conspicuous for his height, isolation, and attire, which bears little relation to the season or decade. Despite the twenty degrees, he wears a too-small blazer over a white shirt, and his signature green cap. In their dark parkas, his tormentors are easy to spot as well. For the moment, they ignore Jerzy, but even from across the street, I can tell that the reason they're hanging back is to instill dread, which for characters like these is half the fun.

The leader and his backup muscle don't sidle over until the bus is a hundred feet away, and this time Jerzy ends up on his knees on the curb and his books end up in a puddle. Once again, Louie and I are too late, and when we cross the street the bus doors are closing. After it pulls away, I notice a man in a wool tweed suit.

"One of your children on the bus?"

"Two," he says.

"Did you see what those kids did to their classmate?"

"Yes."

"Why didn't you say something? I know Jerzy. He's a great kid."

"That's not what I hear from my daughters. You know those kids from Roxbury Farms are troublemakers. He probably asked for it."

Roxbury Farms, a tiny complex of garden apartments, went up at the edge of the neighborhood four years ago. It provides exactly seventeen units of low-income housing, although based on the hysteria at the planning and zoning meetings, you would have thought the town had buried asbestos in our backyard.

"Maybe you should find another place to live," I suggest.

"Why's that?"

"Because you're an asshole."

I would have thought that someone who dresses (did I mention the pocket square?) and behaves like my neighbor would be accustomed to being called an asshole, and through time and repetition, it would have lost the power to offend. Apparently not. His cheeks flush and he throws a wild right hook, which I see coming from a block away. My response is less telegraphed, at least by comparison. It knocks his wind out and doubles him over, and it takes all my restraint not to slip the leather bag off his shoulder into a puddle.

"Whatsa matter?" I ask. "Don't you have cable?"

36

"I SAW THESE KIDS roughing up Jerzy while he was waiting for the bus," I explain. "Jerzy's the boy who shoveled our driveway. It happened two days in a row. The second time, Louie and I crossed the street. The bus was already on its way, but there was a parent standing there who had witnessed the whole thing and did nothing. In fact, he seemed to approve. He looked like the classic investment wanker—wing tips, horn-rimmed glasses, three-piece suit."

"I really don't need a description of his wardrobe," says Sarah.

"He also had a pocket square."

"Travis."

"Okay. I asked him why he just stood there and didn't say anything. He responded by taking a swing at me and I defended myself. This has absolutely nothing to do with the incident in Honolulu."

"He tried to hit you for asking him a question? That seems unlikely. Are you sure that's all you said?"

This second interrogation is conducted in the front seat of Sarah's Jeep outside the headquarters of the Winnetka Police Department. The first, handled by two of Winnetka's finest, was less intense. Louie sits in the ample space between us.

"I may also have called him an asshole."

Although the car is parked, Sarah lays her hands on the steering wheel and drops her head. Her hands, which have delivered hundreds of Winnetkans, are as beautiful as they are skilled, and I fell in love with them approximately ten minutes before the rest of her.

"Travis, are you having a midlife crisis?"

"It's about time, don't you think?"

She twists in the driver's seat and stares at me, as if forming her own diagnosis, and I convince myself that there's an inkling of a smile in her pale green eyes.

"So what are you going to do about Jerzy?"

"I don't know."

"If you don't do anything for him, this is all macho nonsense."

Sarah's smile, if that's what it is, is subtler than the Mona Lisa's, but there's no ambiguity in Louie's eyes. To Louie, there is no such thing as macho nonsense. To him, *everything else* is nonsense, with the notable exception of food, and since my altercation this morning, I'm convinced he's been beaming at me with newfound respect.

My arrest and release make the afternoon paper and are picked up by the wires, and that evening I get calls from both Earl and Stump. Like Sarah, they suspect that I've gone completely off the rails and they don't seem any more reassured by my version of events. The other call, the one from Ponte Vedra, Florida, informing me that my suspension has been extended for the remainder of the year, doesn't come till 11 p.m.

At least I don't have to write that letter.

37

THE NEXT MORNING, I put on my most presentable blazer and one of my few pairs of shoes that don't have spikes sticking out the bottom and drive to New Trier Township High School. Since Elizabeth graduated a decade ago, I've only been back to vote. In fact, pulling a lever in a high school gym every four years is the sum of my input as an American citizen, and that makes coming here to this well-lit administrative office on behalf of a student I barely know all the more unsettling.

Behind the front desk is a human roadblock, whose placard reads: LAURA SKELLCHOCK.

"Laura, good morning. My name is Travis McKinley. I need to talk to someone about a student who's being bullied."

"That's Reece Halsey, our assistant dean. She's out of the office till Friday."

"Can't I talk to someone else?"

"I'm afraid she's the one you need to talk to."

"It can't wait that long, Laura. The kid is getting beat up every morning. He could be dead by then."

"How do you know him?"

"That's the thing. I don't, and that's all the more reason why you should take me seriously."

"I am taking you seriously, Mr. McKinley."

"The only thing I know about him is that he shoveled my driveway and he did a good job and he's a nice kid and he was nice to my son. But even if he did a lousy job on the driveway and was a snotty kid and was mean to my son, he still shouldn't get beat up every morning."

Skellchock responds to this last rhetorical flourish with an eye roll.

"Isn't there a way I can get in touch with his parents? The student's name is Jerzy Solarski. I could also help identify the kids who are involved. The incidents occurred at the bus stop at Downing and Parade. Less than a dozen students get picked up there. It shouldn't be hard to figure out who they are."

The way Skellchock's smile congeals tells me there's something impatient in my tone. The shadow that falls across her eyes bears a frightening resemblance to the one I saw at the Department of Motor Vehicles when someone was insane enough to ask why the line was moving so slowly.

"Aren't you the person who got into the fight with one of our parents?"

"That was unfortunate, but there were no charges."

"Lucky for you, Mr. McKinley. And didn't another fight get you suspended from the Senior Tour?"

"That was also unfortunate."

"Sounds like you're the bully, Mr. McKinley." Then, as suddenly as it arrived, the shadow lifts and her smile softens. "Mr. McKinley, as I'm sure you can appreciate, we can't share information about our students to every nut job who waltzes in here. What I can do is pass your number to Jerzy's parents. If they want to reach out, they will."

"I appreciate that, Laura. Truly."

"My husband's a golfer," she explains.

38

SARAH CAN'T BE THAT mad at me, because that night, she roasts another chicken. Later, as I'm gratefully washing the dishes, I get a call from a woman with a strong Eastern European accent. "This is Rodica Solarski," she says. "Thanks so much for coming to the school today. I can't talk now because I'm at work, but if it's not too late, I could call again during my break."

Instead, I offer to come to her, and an hour later, I retrace my old commute into downtown Chicago. It's been a year and change since Leo Burnett *let me go,* and much longer since I've visited midtown at night. After hours, the district exudes the bristling vigilance of a military installation. Even emptied of workers, it throbs like an enormous machine that never gets switched off.

Rodica's address isn't far from my longtime employer's, and out of morbid curiosity, I walk past the darkened entrance, setting loose the bad old feelings. Three blocks south, still regretting the detour, I enter a massive tower that takes up the entire west side of the block and, escorted by the night guard, ride a chrome-filled elevator high above an inner atrium. "Rodica's the only one on the floor," says the guard.

I slip him a twenty, and he buzzes me through the frosted glass doors. Then I follow the corridor that divides the executive offices and conference rooms that look out over the atrium from the green expanse of shoulder-high cubicles. Parked in front of an open office is a cart laden with cleaning supplies, and in the doorway, a surprisingly delicate woman in her early forties. I hand Rodica the coffee I picked up at the corner and follow her into one of the conference rooms, where we sit at a mahogany table.

"The meeting is called to order," says Rodica, and peels the wax paper off a sandwich brought from home.

"Did Jerzy mention he shoveled my driveway?"

"No. Don't be offended. He rarely talks to me at all."

"We didn't talk much either, but his wit made an impression."

"I think the American term is *wiseass*," says Rodica. Her pale face is framed by jet-black hair cut to her shoulders. Like Jerzy's, her accented English is fluent and precise.

"So did the generous way he treated my five-year-old. That's why I was so disturbed by what I saw at the bus stop. Why do you think they target him, Rodica?"

Rodica shrugs, as if the answer hardly matters. "Because he's too big to be invisible and too soft to fight back," she says. "Because he has an accent and bad skin, and because he's really sweet...."

The mention of her son's kindness causes Rodica's face to crumple. To gather herself, she pries the cap off her coffee and takes a long gulp. "Maybe it's my fault. It was my idea to come here from Bucharest, five years ago—me, Jerzy, and his older sister, Beata. Ironically, I came for the schools. For Jerzy, it's been disastrous from the start, and with Beata graduated, it's much worse. When his sister was here, he at least had someone to sit with at lunch, and she wasn't afraid to confront people."

"Have you spoken to anyone at the school?"

"A waste of time, or, as you Americans like to say—a waste of breath. No one is willing to lift a finger to protect my son. Now his grades have slipped and he's stopped talking. My biggest fear is that he'll do something to harm himself. To be honest, Mr. McKinley, I'm terrified."

Rodica's face crumples again, and now her coffee is finished, so she pushes her hair behind her ears, fits the lid back on the empty cup, and folds the brown paper bag that held her sandwich. "I should get back to work," she says. "Thanks so much for coming and also for the coffee." Before I can respond, she pushes herself away from the table, drops the cup into the garbage bag hanging off the end of her cart, and disappears around the corner.

I head in the opposite direction for a couple of steps, then stop and, for a minute or maybe two, stand there frozen by indecision. Then I head back around the corner and find Rodica in another office.

"Sorry to bother you again. How would you feel if I spent a little time with your son?"

"Doing what?"

"I'm a professional golfer, so I thought maybe I could teach him how to play."

"That sounds wonderful, Mr. McKinley. Golf is all he watches on TV," she says, but her expression is neutral. "I won't mention anything to Jerzy for now. You can surprise him."

On the way to the elevator, I slow to peer into a cubicle very much like the one in which I spent five years. I wonder if Rodica has memorized these snapshots of weddings, babies, graduations, and barbecues.

39

THE BELL IS STILL ringing when Jerzy bursts through a door in the back of the science center and walks with badly concealed haste toward the yellow and black buses lined up on the far side of the parking lot. Although scores of students pour from a dozen buildings, he is as impossible to miss as a giant turtle without a shell. In a sea of affluent preppies, his Eastern European hand-me-downs seem particularly off-kilter, and while Jerzy is certainly uncool, he is also flaunting it. Economic hardship may explain the baggy wool pants and too-small blazer, but not the smiley face T-shirt or Where's Waldo hat. Despite the obvious drawbacks, he can't resist drawing attention to his geeky self. As his own mom points out, he's a wiseass.

If Jerzy hoped to reach the safety of the bus before the Shiny Black Parkas could get a bead on him, it's too late. They're already lying in wait between him and the bus door, and from the front seat of Simon's old pickup, I get my first good look at the brains of the outfit. He's of medium height and wiry, pale and blond, his long bangs cut straight across his forehead. Instead of any outward sign of malevolence, there's something unformed and missing in his features, like the overly symmetrical oval of a child's drawing.

As he waits for Jerzy to get within arm's length, he slips a hand out of his pocket and forms a fist, and as I hop from my truck, I catch myself doing the same. *Be careful. You get in a third fight in a high school parking lot with a bunch of teenagers, Sarah won't be asking any more questions. She'll just put you on meds.*

"Hey, Jerzy," asks the leader softly. "Where you headed?"

As at the bus stop, Jerzy's only resistance is willful denial. He plods ahead as if he doesn't see or hear a thing.

"Over here, you fat fuck."

"Dipshit, he's talking to you."

By now, I'm directly behind the three, and when Buster Blond pulls back his arm, I step in front of him.

"Excuse me, fellas. Don't mean to interrupt, but I need a word with my friend."

For a couple of seconds, the leader stares at me nonplussed, not sure how to react to me or what to do with his fist. When he puts it back in his pocket and steps aside, I guide Jerzy past them to the front seat of Simon's pickup.

40

"You're probably wondering why I'm here," I say.

"Kind of."

"I came to see if you'd like to hit some golf balls."

"Wow," says Jerzy, still digesting his reprieve as his classmates hover nearby. "I guess you really do have a lot of time on your hands."

"As a matter of fact."

"I could probably clear my calendar for the afternoon."

Big Oaks is cold and bleak as Siberia. In every respect, it's the same dreary interior I had to reimagine as Augusta National just to get myself to show up every day, but based on Jerzy's expression you'd think it actually was Augusta. "This place rules," he says, and his eyes delight in every sorry detail, from the ripped Srixon banner advertising a ball they stopped making two years ago, to the corny clock with golf clubs for arms, to the shuddering ball machine.

Once we pick up the clubs and get settled in my stall, I do a quick inventory of what I have to work with. Jerzy, who is at least 6'3" and 220 pounds, is a seventeen-year-old man cub. He has big hands, big feet, and a big head, and the kind of natural size and heft that often translates well to golf. (See: Jack Nicklaus, Craig Stadler, Colin Montgomery, and my old nemesis Stump Peters.) Size gives you ballast that roots you to the ground and, once you learn to shift your weight at the right time, natural power.

I pull the 7-iron from my bag and mold his hands around it until they've glommed into something cohesive. "You want to hold the club very gently," I say. "Whatever you think the pressure should be, it's half that. Okay, now take your hands off and place them back on....All right, now try it again....One more time....That's excellent. Where you've got them now looks really good."

"Thanks, Mr. McKinley. I need to get a grip."

"You and me both...and it's Travis."

I align his feet, tilt him forward into the proper posture, then share a fundamental concept of a good swing, which is to barely swing at all and instead twist your torso back and forth, with your arms going along for the ride. To provide a sense of how it feels when the chest initiates the move, I have him cross his arms and I place my hands on his shoulder, but before I can turn him halfway back, he winces in pain, and when he covers it with a quick smile, I know it's from all the punches he's been taking every morning and afternoon.

"A quarter swing is all we want today. For our purposes, it's better. On the way back, just enough of a turn to get your weight on the inside of your right foot. Then plant the left and turn around it."

I have him rehearse the move several times before I pluck a yellow ball from the basket and place it on the thin mat. Jerzy's first swing is a whiff. So are the second, and the third; and the fourth catches so little of the ball, it doesn't roll off the mat.

The next hour is a blur of shank hooks and shank slices. He hits behind the ball, on top of it, and beside it, and yet, within two thirds of a bucket, I know he has the makings of a golfer. Not because he's flashed an inkling of athletic talent or shown evidence of having absorbed a single thing I've said, but because he is a glutton for punishment. An hour of nonstop frustration and repeated failure rolls off his thick shoulders like rain. Undaunted, he tries as hard on his eighty-eighth swing as his fifty-third and his eleventh. Not only that, he is having fun.

"Keep your grip pressure constant throughout the whole swing," I say, and nudge another Big Oaks rock between his feet. "And try not to get so geeked at the ball. Don't react to it at all. Pretend it isn't there."

"What ball?" he asks.

For the hundredth time, Jerzy pivots and unleashes his abbreviated swing, and for whatever reason (Yahweh, Vishnu, Jesus, grip pressure), the sound of club striking ball is entirely crisper, deeper, and sweeter—and the velocity with which it flies off the face is deliriously disproportionate to the effort put into it. When it drops out of the air and stops rolling, it's traveled more than two football fields.

"Piece of cake," says Jerzy.

41

JERZY SMILES LIKE THE Pope the whole drive home. That's the effect hitting it on the sweet spot has on one's sense of well-being. It smooths out the edges, even the jagged ones. It's like Zen meditation, only better because it isn't bullshit. Although I couldn't be happier for him and even take some credit for his beatific glow, my own state of mind is precarious. I've been uptight since we stashed the clubs at the front desk and headed for Simon's truck, and as I dodge the potholes on Route 38 my unease blooms into something closer to panic.

It started when I placed my hands on Jerzy's shoulders and saw the toll of those punches, and his flinch recalled Rodica's half-smile when I asked about spending time with her son. I realized that the reason she didn't want to tell Jerzy was not to preserve the surprise. It was to protect him from the likelihood that it wouldn't happen at all, that I would have a change of heart or "something would come up" and my impulse to help her kid would evaporate as mysteriously as it arrived.

Rodica's pessimistic scenario didn't pan out. I did show up. Not only that, I snatched him out from under the nose of that little vacant-eyed assassin and introduced him to the wonder that is Big Oaks. But what now?

As I turn onto the street that dead-ends at Roxbury Farms, I think about the bruises on Jerzy's arms and wonder how much of a commitment I'm prepared to make for a goofy teenager who shoveled my driveway and was nice to Noah and whose sardonic wit reminds me of my grandfather. Maybe Rodica knows me better than I know myself, and I'm not cut out to be a do-gooder. If her assessment is accurate and I bail after two or three or four sessions, will that be worse than doing nothing?

And then for some inexplicable reason (Yahweh, Vishnu, Jesus, grip pressure), the anxious voices shut up long enough for me to think, Who knows? And besides that—fuck it.

"So, Jerzy, I've been thinking."

"Uh-oh."

"How about we do this every Tuesday afternoon?"

"Really?"

"Yeah. Really. You'll help me get through my draconian suspension, and I'll teach you a little about golf."

I'm not sure which one of us is more surprised. Or pleased.

42

WHEN I PICK UP Jerzy the following Tuesday, I can tell from his eyes it's been a rough week. I don't know how rough until we get to our stall and Jerzy takes two easy swings with the 7-iron, stops, and looks down at his feet.

"Jerzy, what's the matter?"

"My arms, my shoulders, my ribs. I can't do it."

To be here at Big Oaks and unable to hit a shot is devastating to him, and I don't know what to say. I'm still struggling to come up with plan B when Jerzy hands me the club. "Since I'm so useless, why don't you hit a few? Maybe I can learn by watching."

After a few practice swings, I scoop a ball from the plastic basket with the blade and bounce it into my palm. "You're in for a treat, my friend. Bear in mind that what you're about to see is on a whole different level from just hitting balls."

"I'll try."

"When I have to describe to the layman what it is that I do, I often fall back on the language of art. To put it simply, I use my clubs to paint pictures."

"Let me see if I grasp the analogy," says Jerzy. "The irons, woods, and putter are brushes. The ball is the paint, this stall the easel or studio, and the golf course, or in this case Big Oaks, is your canvas."

"Very good."

"And you're Picasso."

"Hey, you said it, not me."

"Paint away, Pablo."

My first two swings are Jerzyesque. I don't whiff—I'm a former U.S. Senior Open champion, for Christ's sake— but like him, I get too amped, hold the club too tight, and the result is two ground balls.

"Maybe you need to loosen up. Or is this your blue period?"

"That's an excellent suggestion. Thank you."

I bend at the waist, windmill my arms, and swivel my hips. "A routine I picked up from my amigo Miguel Ángel Jiménez," I say. Despite the elaborate stretching and Castilian lisping, my third shot rolls harmlessly off-line. On my fourth, I finally make a good pass at it. It produces a hard hook that never gets five feet off the ground and misses my target by inches.

"I get it," says Jerzy, almost smiling, "you're trying to hit the guy in that lunar vehicle picking up balls."

"It's not easy being a role model," I concede. "There's a lot of pressure and responsibility. And, in case you haven't noticed, that thing is moving."

Which is why I consider my next salvo—a vicious slice that bores in on the buggy like a heat-seeking missile before scoring a direct hit on the front door—one of the two or three best shots in my career, and as the driver slams on the brakes, I improvise an understated victory dance, which goes on for minutes and owes heavy debts to the WWF and *Soul Train*.

"Good thing you stretched," says Jerzy.

The guy behind the wheel, who is being bombarded while picking up balls at minimum wage, is less enthused. "McKinley, you do that again," he shouts, "I'm going to come up there and kick your ass."

43

THE CAGED BUGGY, WHICH had drawn perilously close, makes a U-turn and goes back to collecting Big Oaks range rocks.

"Jerzy, I'm sorry you couldn't swing the club today, but we're going to make a golfer out of you, I promise."

"Turn me into a Cheez Doodle for all I care. As long it's something other than Jerzy Solarski—dipshit, fat fuck, pizza face, loser, and one other thing, what is it? Oh, yeah, Polack."

"When I'm through with you, you'll be Jerzy Solarski—dipshit, fat fuck, pizza face, loser, Polack, golfer. How does that sound?"

"Better."

And that should have been enough for me. Thankfully, it's been a while since Elizabeth and Simon passed through the pricklier stages of adolescence, yet not so long that I've forgotten that conversation with a teen is a mine-field. If you are able to extract a glimmer of a smile from a seventeen-year-old, you've done a full day's work. Time to go home, crack a beer, and put your feet up, but I'm so relieved about having salvaged the afternoon, I prattle on like a twit.

"I hope you realize that not a single thing those morons are calling you is accurate. You're a big dude, but you're hardly fat. You're no bigger than Jack Nicklaus was at your age, and he's only the best golfer of all time. You're not a loser, your skin issues are minor and temporary, and you're not a dipshit, whatever that is, and the last I checked, you can't be a Polack, if you're not from Poland. Although I suppose they could make an exception."

"How did you know I'm not Polish?"

"Your mom told me that she and your sister and you came here from Rumania."

"When did you talk to her?"

"A few days ago. I couldn't show up at school and pick you up without running it by her."

"Why didn't she tell me? Was this some plan she dreamed up to boost my self-esteem?"

"The reason she didn't tell you was because she was afraid I wouldn't follow through and then you'd be disappointed. Your mom had zero to do with this. Believe me, she has enough on her plate."

"What is that supposed to mean? What do you know about her plate?"

"Not much."

"Exactly," he says, and lumbers off in the direction of the bathroom. While he's gone I work my way through the bucket with the 7-iron and berate myself for having learned so little in half a century. After ten minutes, he still hasn't returned, and after fifteen, I realize he's not going to. I reach the parking lot in time to see him step onto an eastbound bus.

44

THE FOLLOWING TUESDAY, I'M back in the New Trier parking lot waiting on Jerzy and the bell, and once again, I'm not alone. Till now, I'd never appreciated the commitment, discipline, and punctuality required to be a top-notch high school bully. Less motivated sociopaths-in-training would be in the library reading a muscle mag or carving sinister symbols into a desk. Instead, they're out here freezing their asses off behind the maintenance shed and choreographing their next ambush.

My rivals are conscientious, but I have the element of surprise. This morning I persuaded Sarah to swap cars, so that while I keep an eye on the boys in black, they take no notice of the green Jeep or the man behind the wheel, his face buried in the afternoon paper.

From my reading, I learn that the Trevian hoopsters

dropped their ninth straight last night to archrival West Hill. The photograph shows West Hill's Dave Bond scoring over a New Trier player with distinctive straight bangs named Brune Pickering, and according to the box score, Pickering led the losers with eleven points and seven assists. Is that all it takes to become a total shit?—be the best player on an awful basketball team, and be saddled at birth with the name Brune? Whatever.

When the bell goes off, I close the paper and scan the exits. This afternoon, Jerzy makes his retreat from the study hall. While the Parkas move to intercept him at the end of the walkway, I roll up from the other side of the lot, moving slowly so as not to be noticed.

As I inch along, I study Jerzy's face and body language and am encouraged by what I don't see. There are no fresh wounds on his face or neck, and his gait doesn't favor one side or the other. Wishful thinking, maybe, but I also detect a new bounce in his step and a hint of defiance.

Unaware that anyone else is eyeing their prey, the boys take their time. That allows me to slip in front of them just before Jerzy reaches the end of the walkway. When Pickering spots me, I've already reached across and opened the front door and called out in an urgent whisper, "Hey, Jerzy, it's me. Get in."

Jerzy is so close the front door nearly hits him, yet

nothing in his expression indicates he sees me. The blank mask he adopts for his tormentors is now aimed at me. Instead of climbing into the safety of the Jeep and heading to Big Oaks, he walks directly past the car into a whirlwind of flying fists.

45

THREE DAYS LATER, I'M back at New Trier again. This time I park and walk around to the main entrance, where I inform the guard I have an appointment with the assistant dean of students, Reece Halsey. On the way to Halsey's office, I must make a wrong turn, because instead of entering the administrative wing, I find myself in a wide hallway lined with classrooms. The classrooms are empty and so is the corridor, but the tin lockers and low water fountains drum up a parade of ancient memories, mostly lousy.

When the corridor ends, I turn in the direction of the noise, which grows more urgent with each step till I push through a pair of doors into a vast rotunda. The multicolored flags of every nation, presumably including Rumania, hang from the high ceiling, and to my left is a stack of faded green plastic trays. I grab a tray and a plate and watch a woman wearing a hairnet ladle something brown onto something white. Then I slide the tray over the rails, fill a paper cup with something pink, and face the din.

The cafeteria must hold a thousand students. Nine hundred and ninety-nine of them crowd around a hundred tables, and one, his jug head tilting toward the straw in a carton of milk, sits alone, surrounded by empty chairs.

"What are you doing here?" he asks.

"I hear the chef does an amazing beef stew."

"Yeah," says Jerzy. "He opens the can."

As I take my first bite, a wet napkin lands with a splat at the center of our table, setting off a round of laughter.

"There's something I want to tell you, which I haven't shared with anyone in thirty-five years. Not my wife, my kids, or my best friend. Not even Louie."

"Louie?"

"My dog. I believe you two have met."

Half a muffin hits the table, followed by several packets of salt and pepper. I open one of each, sprinkle them on the stew, and take another bite.

"In eighth grade, the same shit happened to me. At that point, I was as tall as I am now, absurdly skinny, braces, glasses, an all-round winning look. This kid named Rudy Laplante, who happened to be the scion of a huge trucking company, decided he was going to make my life miserable, and for several months did a thorough job. At one point, my mother found out what was happening. You know what she said I should do?"

"No."

"I guess you wouldn't, since I haven't told you yet. Take a chair and smash it over his head."

"Did you?"

"What do you think? But I've always been grateful for the suggestion."

"Just as well. You could have fractured his skull. How would your mother have felt then?"

"You know, I've wondered about that. One possibility is that she knew I wasn't capable of it. The other is that she didn't give a shit. Figured that was Rudy's problem. I prefer that one."

"You saying I should smash a chair over Pickering's head?"

"In your case, that probably wouldn't be a good idea, although I'd love to watch, if you did. In fact, I'd pay to watch."

The aerial assault picks up and the incoming turns healthier—grapes, pineapple cubes, an apple core, a banana—and Jerzy and I ignore it all, having reached an unspoken agreement not to give the assholes the satisfaction. More miraculous than the manna from heaven is the arrival at our table of another student. She is small and thin and wears a black Smashing Pumpkins T-shirt over a black vintage dress, with black nail polish and black lipstick. In addition to being monochromatic and brave, she's pretty.

"Welcome to Pariahville," says Jerzy. "Population three. I hope you brought an umbrella."

"You're funny," says the girl.

"I think you mean funny-looking."

"No, I mean *funny*," she says with a touch of impatience. "As in witty. And I like your blazer. Very Angus in AC/DC. All you need is the shorts."

You're right, that's all he needs. But I appreciate the sentiment. To me she looks like a black angel.

"So, Jerzy, we good?"

"Yeah."

"See you next week, then," I say, and wielding my tray like a shield, I head for the exit.

46

THE FOLLOWING WEEK WHEN we return to Big Oaks, Jerzy grabs the 7-iron and swings without discomfort. Pain-free, his move is as long and loose as Sam Snead's.

"Pickering's appendix burst," explains Jerzy. "He's been out all week and could be out for a month." I would rather have heard he's on life support, but I'll take it.

"How about that wonderful girl? Any more interaction with her?"

"Which girl?"

"Don't give me that 'which girl.' The one who joined you at lunch."

"Lyla," says Jerzy. "Of course not. That was a once-in-a-lifetime event, like Halley's Comet."

"She likes you."

"That's a physical impossibility. As far as I know, she's not blind."

"She's not. She commented on your attire. Favorably. In any case, between Pickering's appendix and Lyla's Comet, I'd say things are looking up. I propose we show our gratitude, up the ante, and go to work."

That afternoon, we spend almost four hours in the stall. Jerzy makes so much progress, we decide to come back the next afternoon and Thursday, and in our third session, Jerzy has a breakthrough that most golfers never do. He learns how to "save it for the bottom," as in connect his considerable size and heft to the bottom of his swing where the club meets the ball, the only part that matters. It sounds like a shotgun and turns every head on the range.

"That was stupid long," I say as his 3-wood bounces off that old Srixon banner. "At least thirty yards longer than I hit that club."

"You're not exactly a spring chicken, Travis."

"True. I'm a September chicken."

Over the next couple of days, he tattoos the old banner so many times that it finally gives up the ghost, detaches from the wire curtain, and flutters to the ground. "I can't tell you how long I've been waiting to see that," I say. "Like Berliners when the wall came down."

The bigger revelation comes a week later, when I hand him my old bull's-eye putter and walk him to the green rectangle about the size of three parking spaces which they have the temerity to call a putting green. I don't know if it's up there with Harvey Penick and Ben Crenshaw at Austin Country Club, but I'll never forget the first time I see Jerzy roll it on the Big Oaks cement.

Putting is two things—aim and feel. Aim is the easy part. With practice, almost any asshole can do it. Feel, sensing how hard to strike a putt to make it roll the desired distance, is more elusive and nearly impossible to teach. After giving him a chance to get acclimated to the speed, approximately like putting on a bowling alley, I drop a tee ten feet away and ask him to stop the ball beside it. When that proves a minor challenge, I drop four more at three-foot intervals, then place five balls at his feet and ask him to roll each one to the next farther tee. When he's done, I realize I've underestimated his potential.

"Jerzy, I got some good news. You can hit it long and you can putt. If you can do both, you can play. As in really play."

47

By now, it's the third week of March, and that weekend a lovely thing happens. It gets warmer. That Saturday and Sunday it soars into the high thirties, causing the snow to lose a bit of its grip and giving the ground a chance to thaw. Monday morning, it's back into the twenties again, but by then it's too late. When I pick up Jerzy at school that afternoon, Louie sits beside me on the front seat.

"I don't think they allow dogs in Big Oaks," says Jerzy.

"They don't allow dogs where we're going, either, but since no one will be there, it's not going to be a problem."

Instead of the haul up 38, we make the shorter trip to Creekview Country Club, where, with half the course still under snow, the lot is empty.

"It's time to go golfing," I say as we hop out of the car. "I got one of my old bags and put together a set for you.

I've got literally hundreds of clubs in my basement. It's really no big deal."

"It is to me, Travis. Thanks."

"My pleasure," I say, then reach into the trunk for the Big Oaks caps I bought that morning. "This is so we don't forget where we came from."

"Representing," says Jerzy as we doff our new caps.

With Louie trotting behind us, we make the short walk to the practice range, where we hit and shag a dozen balls apiece. Then we roll a few on the muddy practice green.

"This is your first round of golf," I say. "That's a big deal, so we're going to play for real. Because of the conditions, it's got to be lift, clean, and place, which means we can pull the ball out of the muck, wipe it off, and place it in a playable spot, but we're going to write down every stroke, and when we're done, we're going to add them all up. Golf is a number. That's all it is, and the only way to see if we're on the right track is to keep score. So as my grandfather used to say, 'No gimmes, no mulligans, no bullshit, let's play golf.'"

Despite the twenty-eight degrees, the three of us enjoy a lovely afternoon, and it occurs to me that when it comes to golf, Twain got it exactly wrong. Rather than *a good walk spoiled*, it's a crappy walk made bearable. Golf takes what would otherwise be a tedious eight-mile hump, marred with far too much self-reflection, and makes it interesting. Just because you don't know the name of every tree and bird, and couldn't care less, doesn't mean you don't appreciate being outside, feeling the breeze on your skin and the ground underfoot. And just because you have a little hand-eye coordination, that doesn't make you a lightweight.

Jerzy, it turns out, has more than his share of hand-eye coordination, and although he hits four bad shots for every good one, he takes pleasure in them all, just like that first afternoon at Big Oaks. Pop would have appreciated that, the same with Jerzy's brisk pace of play, which allows us to get around in two hours and finish before the sun disappears. On 18, Jerzy rolls in a twelve-footer for 117, and we tilt our caps and shake hands.

"Thanks, Travis. What a wonderful day. I'm only sorry I didn't get a chance to meet your grandfather."

"You met him eighteen times. His ashes were sprinkled on every green."

We get in two more rounds that week and, with Pickering still recuperating, three more the following. Along the way, Jerzy's scores dip steadily—116, 109, 97, 88, 83, and when I pick him up the following Monday, I feel like he's got a legitimate chance to break 80, particularly with the breeze down and the temperature hovering around forty. Unfortunately, his right eye is swollen shut.

"I take it Pickering has made a full recovery."

"Correct."

"What are you doing Sunday?"

"Watching the Masters, of course."

"Then come over and watch it with us."

In case you're interested, here's the scorecard from Jerzy's first round of golf:

Creekview Country Club

HOLE	PAR	JERZY	TRAV:S	HOLE	PAR	JERZY	TRAV:S
1	4	6	4	10	4	6	4
2	5	11	4	11	4	7	3
3	4	5	4	12	4	8	4
4	4	5	5	13	5	6	5
5	3	4	2	14	4	6	4
6	5	8	5	15	3	5	3
7	4	8	4	16	4	5	4
8	3	7	4	17	3	5	3
9	4	6	4	18	5	9	5
OUT	36	60	36	TOTAL	72	117	71

SCORER: *Travis McKinly* ATTEST: _____ DATE: _____

48

THE HEAVYSET KID WHO knocks on my door Sunday afternoon looks discouragingly like the one who arrived two months earlier. He wears the same heavy green sweater and black wool trousers and, instead of a gash on his forehead, sports a Technicolor shiner from the same source, which in the last couple of days has bloomed purple green. My only discernible influence is the Big Oaks cap.

Inside the entryway, there's the usual stunted male reception—a sniff from Louie, a too-cool-for-school "Hey" from Noah, and an inspired "Come on in" from the reigning patriarch. Thank God Sarah comes running from the kitchen and throws her arms around the kid, or else he'd never know how glad we all are to see him inside our house.

The initial awkwardness behind us, we head to the den,

where, with snacks and beverages at hand, we hunker down for the afternoon. Final-round coverage has just begun, and Jim Nantz, in his third year at the helm, sets the scene. After nine holes, Couples, the leader from day one, is still out in front at eight under par, one better than Mark O'Meara and three better than David Duval, but the story of the morning is Jack Nicklaus, who birdied four out of his first seven holes and at fifty-eight is making yet another run.

"You've got plenty of time," says Jerzy. "He's six years older than you."

"Yeah. And he's Jack Nicklaus. Besides, I don't look good in green."

For the next several hours, we luxuriate in the dependable pleasures and smarmy eccentricities of golf's most polished telecast. With the tinkling soundtrack underneath, Nantz walks us across the Hogan and Nelson Bridges, discourses on the swirling winds of Golden Bell, and points out the Sarazen plaque and the Eisenhower tree, the only thing all afternoon that gets a rise out of Louie. For longtime viewers like us, the familiar bits of lore and language—*Amen Corner, Firethorn, the pine straw, the patrons*—are like the refrains in a secular hymnal. Through it all, there's the stunning seminatural beauty and the blissfully few commercials.

"Ever play Augusta?" asks Jerzy.

"Only in his mind," says Noah for me.

"When I become a member, you and Noah will be my first two guests," says Jerzy.

"Can't wait," says Noah.

After Nicklaus falls back, it's a three-man race to the wire between Couples, Duval, and O'Meara. Couples is the most beloved and Duval the most feared, yet it's the chubby-faced O'Meara, who till now has been best known for his friendship with Tiger, who stands over a seventeen-footer for birdie on the last hole to win it all. No one thinks for a second he'll sink it. Instead, there will be polite oohs and ahhs as his putt slides barely off-line, and the three will head back to 11, aka White Dogwood, for the play-off. O'Meara, however, refuses to follow the script. He hits one of the great putts in Masters history and pours it into the heart.

If this were a normal stop on the PGA tour, it would end right now with a wife and toddlers in his arms, but because it's the Masters, *a tradition like no other,* it's on to Butler Cabin. There, with a fire crackling in the background and Hootie Johnson, the chairman of Augusta National, presiding, last year's winner, Tiger Woods, helps his friend into a 43 regular.

When the telecast ends, I lend Jerzy the book on Augusta that I got from my grandfather and give him a ride home, the two of us still buzzing from the purity and finality of O'Meara's putt.

"I've always been a sucker for underdogs," I say.

"Me too," says Jerzy. "I wonder why."

Fired up by O'Meara's courage and galled by the spectacle of Jerzy's right eye, I blurt out a reckless offer:

"The next time Pickering hits you, you hit him back twice as hard. *Or* you ask Lyla on a date. Do either one, I don't care which, and I'll take you to Augusta."

49

THREE DAYS LATER, I take my place in the New Trier parking lot with even more trepidation than usual. By dangling a round at Augusta as a reward, I put a bounty on Pickering's head, and if by some wonderful chance Jerzy takes me up on it and comes out on top in a big way, I could be an accessory to assault, the point of no return for Finchem, if not Sarah. However, it's the more likely scenarios that have kept me up at night, which are that as a result of my grandiose meddling, Jerzy gets the crap kicked out of him, or his heart stomped. Or both.

You can imagine my relief when I see Jerzy's jug head, looking no worse for wear, bobbing above the stream of students that pours out of the back of the science building. Spotting Lyla nearby further bolsters my spirits. I try not to make too much of this—after all, they're not interacting—until I notice the shorts. He is not wearing golf shorts or tennis shorts or gym shorts but the black wool variety, which Lyla said was the one minor detail separating him from the lead guitarist of AC/DC. As I mull the ramifications of Jerzy taking fashion cues from his Goth classmate, Pickering and his posse zero in.

As always, Jerzy acts as if he doesn't see them, but Lyla, as befits someone in a black jumpsuit, ripped stockings, and army boots, is more combative. She curses Pickering out, and now it's Pickering who looks away, as flummoxed by this outburst of female ferocity as Jerzy was with him. When Lyla gets in his face, he still won't meet her eye, so Lyla, who weighs about ninety pounds with her boots on, shoves him with both hands.

After an awkward shrug toward his cronies, Pickering pushes Lyla back, and although Pickering's response is halfhearted and gentle by comparison, it's not gentle enough for Jerzy, who hauls off and smacks him in the face. I know it's a slap and not a punch because of the sound, which is very similar to one of his flushed 3-woods.

With the sound still echoing in the parking lot, Pickering and his cronies jump Jerzy, and for ten seconds it looks like three dogs attacking a bear. I hop from the truck, but before I get much closer, a tiny ragtag militia races to Jerzy's defense. One sports a tartan skirt fastened with a big brass pin, the other a patriotic Mohawk dyed red, white, and blue, and although neither is much bigger than Lyla, they are enough to turn the tide, and when two teachers and a guard pry them apart, Pickering and company are more relieved than outraged.

To the victors go the spoils, and for several minutes the three beam and strut while accepting the plaudits of a jubilant throng of misfits. Then Jerzy excuses himself from the celebration and wanders over.

"I guess you're wondering why I went with a slap instead of a punch," he asks.

"Based on the sound, I'm glad you did."

"The last thing I want to do is break my hand now," he says with a poorly suppressed grin.

"I gather you had already asked Lyla out."

"Correct," says Jerzy, his face turning approximately as red as Pickering's after impact.

"Well done. Two for two. I'll start making some calls."

50

Two weeks later, Jerzy and I walk out of the sleepy Augusta Regional Airport with our sticks in tow. Parked at the curb is an azure-blue '74 Eldorado convertible, antelope horns sprouting from the grille and Creedence's "Born on the Bayou" blaring from the stereo. Behind the wheel is Stump and beside him is Earl, and both seem to be relishing their morning cigars.

"Are you going to stand there gawking at the man's ride," asks Earl, "or you going to get in?"

We do the latter and desist with the former, or is it the other way around? I can never remember. In any case, we're soon loping down a Georgia two-lane on a perfect late-April day, the wind in our hair, the sun on our faces, and the smoke in our eyes. At the city line, Jerzy taps me on the elbow and points at the large roadside sign: WELCOME TO AUGUSTA, GEORGIA, HOME OF THE MASTERS, but

I can't say that it fills me with the same giddy anticipation.

Even before I left Jerzy and Lyla in the parking lot that afternoon, I began to compile a list of people I could call who might be susceptible to groveling. As you might imagine, the list wasn't long and my connection to most of it tenuous. To give you an idea, I even put in a call to my good pal Marcus Azawa, chairman and CEO of Azawa Industries, based entirely on the enthusiasm with which he shook my hand before the play-off in Hawaii. Unfortunately, with Marcus and everyone else I contacted, my reputation preceded me. Even Stump, who might otherwise have been able to wangle an invite, was tainted by association, and Earl wasn't going to be of much help prying open the gates of an institution that didn't accept its first African-American till 1990 and where until 1983 all the caddies were black.

Stump turns off the main drag, and with the V-8 gurgling beneath the endless hood, rolls up Washington Road. At 2604, he pulls over so we can all peer through what looks like a tunnel but is in fact a canopy of branches formed by the sixty surviving magnolias planted from seeds by Prosper Berckmans a century and a half ago. In the light at the far end, behind a circle of grass and a flagpole, are the steps of a simple white plantation-style house, and walking past it is a man in white overalls and a green cap. Just off our chrome bumper is a sign that reads PRIVATE PROPERTY. NO TRESPASSING.

"Magnolia Lane," says Stump through his cigar smoke, "the most famous address in golf and the object of all hope and desire. We're not going in now—you can't just hop on a track like Augusta National after eight hours in airplanes and rental cars—but I thought you might want to see it from the front as God intended."

What is needed first, according to Stump, is a tune-up, which is why he's taken the liberty of booking a tee time at a course nearby. Stump isn't exaggerating about the proximity, and less than two minutes later he noses the Caddy through the gates of the Augusta Country Club and pulls up to a clubhouse at least as impressive as the one at the end of Magnolia Lane.

Since this is a warm-up, we forgo the range and the putting green and head directly to the first tee, where we take a couple of minutes to stretch our mostly middle-aged bodies in the Georgia sun.

"Jerzy, I know it's got to be intimidating," says Stump, "to share the tee box with two household names and a journeyman."

"Intimidating?" says Jerzy with a bit of Rumanian in the vowels. "I feel like I stumbled into an AARP convention."

"Well, let's see how you feel in an hour, motherfucker," says Stump, but Earl snorts his approval.

"Where the hell you find this kid, Travis?"

"In the neighborhood."

"Really?" says Earl. "He seems too interesting for your neighborhood."

With Stump serving as obscene MC, we enjoy a raucous couple of hours, but when we reach the 9th fairway even Stump falls silent. To the left of our carts are a stand of pines and, beyond them, shimmering in the afternoon light, the dazzling emerald of another fairway, a pair of greens, and a sliver of water.

"Jerzy, you know what that is?" asks Stump.

"Of course, Mr. Stump. It's Amen Corner. And why are you whispering?"

51

AFTER WE HOLE OUT, I thank Stump and Earl and let them know we'll see them in three and a half hours. Exactly. Then I walk to the cart and pull off my bag.

"Jerzy, grab your sticks."

"Why?"

"A deal is a deal. I told you that if you stood up to Pickering or asked out Lyla, I'd take you to Augusta National, and you did both. Since I couldn't get us an engraved invitation, we'll have to be a little more proactive. Besides, fuck 'em if they can't take a joke."

"I don't think they can," says Jerzy, unfastening his bag and following me into the woods, where we soon reach the stone wall that marks the boundary between the two courses. From there, we can hear the water flowing through Rae's Creek and see two golfers and their caddies on the right side of the 11th green.

"Take a joke, I mean," continues Jerzy softly. "I don't think they have a sense of humor about any of this—the patrons, the cabins, the green jackets, the trees, *the tradition like no other*. I don't think they have a sense of humor about one blade of their bent or Bermuda grass. In fact, they might shoot us on sight."

"Which is why we can't get caught."

I remove my Big Oaks cap and stuff it between my irons. Then I unzip the side pocket of my bag and pull out a large manila envelope addressed to me. Jammed into the right-hand corner are more than two dozen stamps, and in the other is a return address in Birmingham, Alabama. "A gift from a friend named Owl," I say.

I run a finger under the flap and pull out an immaculate pair of white overalls. On the right chest pocket is the insignia of Augusta National—the outline of the continental United States with a red flag sticking out of the approximate spot where we are now. Since Owl is a man known for his fastidious attention to detail, the envelope also contains an official green Masters cap, a scorecard, a yardage book, and a pencil.

"Aren't you going to play?"

"Not today, Jerzy."

As I step into my new uniform, I take another look at Jerzy's. The same afternoon I called Owl, who then got in touch with his cousin, a former Augusta National caddy,

Jerzy and I took a trip to Brooks Brothers, where I bought him a pair of pink seersucker shorts, a white polo shirt, and a pale blue cashmere sweater, each preppy item carefully selected to suggest the social ease of someone who is not only well off but has been so for generations. Overall, Jerzy carries off his new look pretty well, I think. The only thing I couldn't talk him out of is the Big Oaks cap, which as far as I know, he hasn't taken off since I gave it to him.

After two putts apiece, neither golfer on 11 is any closer to the hole, which gives me time to stash my clubs and confirm that there is not another group coming up right behind the twosome. When the golfers and their caddies clear the green, we clamber over the wall, take off our shoes and socks, and wade across the icy stream.

52

UNDER ANY CIRCUMSTANCES, YOUR first steps on Augusta National are going to be overwhelming. That ours are heading in the wrong direction on the 11th fairway only makes them more so. On one hand, the scene is achingly familiar, since I've watched drives bounding down this fairway countless times on countless telecasts. On the other, there's the shock of actually being here in person and feeling the sacred televised sod pushing up through the soles of our shoes. Then, on top of everything else, there's the darker thrill of being uninvited and being here anyway.

"Jerzy, what do you think?"

"I'm not sure I can."

"Well, to paraphrase Julius, we've crossed our creek. There's no turning back now."

"I assume you mean Caesar, not Boros," he says.

"Correct."

To settle my nerves, I focus on my job, which is to guide Jerzy around this course in as few strokes as possible, and as we head up the fairway, I pull out the scorecard and fold it to the back nine. "We're starting on eleven," I offer, "aka White Dogwood, a long par four. Where we're walking now is about where you want to land your drive." And when we reach the tee box, I pluck a couple of blades of grass, and rather than pocket them as souvenirs, feed them to the warm breeze.

"So what do we got?" asks Jerzy, looking over my shoulder at the card.

"A bit of a dilemma."

"A little late for that, isn't it, Emperor?"

"I mean which tees do we play. From the championship tees, the ones used by O'Meara, Couples, and Duval, the course plays a robust sixty-five hundred yards. For the members, it's a more manageable sixty-one hundred, but as you know, we're not members, and are unlikely to ever be members, so I don't feel quite right playing their tees."

"You saying we should play this puppy from the tips?"

"Why not? We came all this way, inhaled all that airplane air. Let's find out what the fuss is about. Get our money's worth, so to speak."

"Works for me," says Jerzy with a grin.

"Good." I hand him the driver and slap a new Titleist in his palm, the initials *J* and *S* written with a blue Sharpie on each side of the red 3, but as he bends to tee it up, I hear voices, and they're growing louder.

53

WHEN I LOOK OVER my shoulder, a golf cart, containing two large men and no golf clubs, is barreling directly toward us. Rather than your standard E-Z-GO, it has four rows of seats. It's the kind of all-purpose vehicle used to transport golfers back to their respective holes after a rain delay, or, to cite just one more example, to whisk a pair of trespassing miscreants off the premises, and that's where the burliness of the occupants comes in. Both look like they could have played Division I football while moonlighting as bouncers, and one of them has a walkie-talkie in his hand.

Despite evoking Caesar so recently, I look back over my shoulder toward Rae's Creek, but there's no point making a run for it. Not with Jerzy's sticks on my back and them in a cart. *We're going to get kicked off the course while our feet are still damp,* and my last coherent wish is for Jerzy to hit the goddamned ball so that after all the humiliation, career damage, and legal fallout, we'll at least have that one shot at Augusta to burnish in our memories, but now the cart is parked beside us and it's too late even for that.

"My apologies for the interruption," says the driver. "We'll be out of your way in a second." Then he touches the brim of his cap and keeps on going.

54

"THAT WAS AEROBIC," I say as the cart disappears over the hill and the palpitations in my chest subside.

"Thank God for Owl," says Jerzy.

"True. To recap and regroup, we're on number eleven, aka White Dogwood. It looks tight from the tee, but as you saw on the way here, it opens up. It's not as hard as it looks."

This is not entirely true. By the luck of real estate and geography, we're starting our round on the second-hardest hole on the course, but I see no point in sharing that, and my tact is rewarded when Jerzy steps up and pipes his first drive straight down the middle.

"Golf shot, Jerzy. Let's go find it."

When we do, I see why the hole plays so hard. After a perfect drive, Jerzy has 207 yards, from a hook lie to a green with water left.

"Anything right of the flag is great," I say. "Even right of the green. Anything left is in the water. And don't be afraid to take a divot. It's just a golf course. The grass will grow back."

Despite my assurances, Jerzy hits a top, which might actually be lucky, because it takes the water out of play and still rolls within fifteen yards of the green. Before he attempts the chip, we walk up the bank to get our first good look at an Augusta National green, whose contours and color are so dramatic they seem extraterrestrial. Apparently the grass really is greener on the other side.

"It's like walking on the moon," says Jerzy.

"One small step for Jerzy Solarski. One giant leap for golfkind."

Jerzy thins his chip, too, leaving himself a forty-five-footer, straight downhill with at least nine feet of break. But as you may recall, Jerzy can roll his rock. He taps it as delicately as you might nudge a beloved snoring grandfather at the Thanksgiving table, and the ball tracks perfectly end over end, takes the break, and on its last half-turn, topples into the hole.

"These greens are fast," says Jerzy. "But they're not Big Oaks fast."

55

AFTER ONE OF THE better opening pars in the under-documented history of golf trespassing, we soldier on to Golden Bell, perhaps the most whispered-over 155 yards on earth. If you've ever owned a television, you know too much about this nasty little par 3 with the bank in front that funnels anything short into the creek, the traps and flower beds that catch anything long, and the inscrutable winds that make it so hard to avoid one or the other.

Months of airtime have been devoted to the breeze alone, and while I've learned that Hogan studied the leaves on a certain branch of a certain tree, and Snead looked at some other bit of foliage, while Nelson and Nicklaus looked somewhere else again, none of that is the least bit helpful. Neither is the one thing I can remember with certainty, which is that you can't go by what the flag is doing.

"We just got out of Rae's Creek," I say as I hand Jerzy the 6. "We don't want to be in it again."

As I feared, it turns out to be a club and a half too much, and after chipping out of the azaleas, Jerzy walks off with his first bogey.

56

THAT SETS THE PATTERN of par/bogey golf, which Jerzy somehow maintains for the next hour. On the par-five 13th, he reaches the green in regulation and two putts for par, and on 14, the most wildly contoured green on the course, he rolls in a side-hill twelve-footer to steal bogey. Two putts from fifty feet earn him another par on 16, and despite catching a piece of the Eisenhower tree off the tee, he manages to bogey 17.

I'd describe these holes in more detail, but you know what they look like as well as me. Instead, let me try to convey what it's like to experience them in the flesh. I've mentioned the colors and the contours of the greens, and I'm sure you've heard about the drastic changes in elevation, all of which are impossible to appreciate on television, but the biggest difference, between Augusta today and all those afternoons in my den, between

Augusta standing up and Augusta sitting down, is the silence.

You want an idea of what it's like to play Augusta on your own, watch the Masters on mute. With no applause from the patrons, no roars through the pines, no microphones on the tees, and no blather from the tower. When we walk over the Hogan Bridge to the 12th green, we do it without Nantz murmuring sweet reverential nothings in our ears, and when we traverse the Nelson Bridge to the 13th fairway, there's no cocktail music underneath.

It's just the course, the pines, the sky, and...oh, yeah...us, and no offense to CBS, this is better. So much so that it's all going too quickly, and before I know it, Jerzy has backed up a solid drive through the chute on 18 with an even better iron to the green and tapped in for his fourth par in eight holes.

I know what you're thinking. How can a kid who didn't pick up a club till three months ago par half his holes at Augusta National? From the back tees? Certainly, it's unlikely, and I'm surprised too, but it's not like we haven't all brought home the occasional unlikely score now and then. In any case, let me explain how Jerzy's been getting it done. Some of it might even be helpful the next time you tee it up.

First of all, Jerzy is a big kid with a real golf swing. When he catches it right, it flies as far and high as a top college player's. He only does that about a fifth of the time, but when he does, either off the tee or from the fairway, it gives him a chance for a par. Another twenty percent of his shots are "good misses," pushes or pulls that fly within fifteen yards of his target, and at least today, so far, they haven't led to big numbers. The same is true with his god-awful shots, and that's been the biggest key today. Jerzy's most frequent miss is a hard top, and on these fairways, they roll forever.

The truth is that in some ways, Augusta plays surprisingly easy. The fairways are enormous, there isn't a blade of rough, and when you hit into the trees, there's almost always room to advance the ball. What is hard is the greens, and Jerzy is a Rumanian-American Crenshaw. After his first day at Big Oaks, he was a better putter than me, and after a week, he was better than two thirds of the guys on the Senior Tour.

Another factor in Jerzy's favor, if I say so myself, is that he's got yours truly on the bag. For example, forty minutes ago on 13, after he pushed his drive into the pine straw. Even though he only had 201 to the green and a direct shot, I refused to turn over the 4-iron and made him chip out. With all the chances we've taken to be here, you might think it's odd to be conservative now, but to me the two are unrelated. The only thing that matters in this game is the score, something hackers never quite understand, even when they think they do. If you can't make a shot eighty percent of the time and there's a penalty if you don't, you shouldn't try it. Ever. No matter where you are.

Finally, please bear in mind, you did buy a book with the word *miracle* in the title.

57

THEY SAY THE MASTERS doesn't start till the back nine on Sunday. It may even be true, but it doesn't apply when you play on a Wednesday and start on 11. In our particular circumstances, the critical stretch isn't the back nine or the front, it's the precarious stroll we're about to take now from the 18th green to the first tee. This exposed fifty-yard perp walk, which leads between the practice green and the back of the clubhouse, where a cocktail party is in full bloom, is *our* Amen Corner, and the prayer that comes to mind is the one from Sunday school about forgiving *our trespasses, as we forgive those who trespass against us.*

Lured by this lovely weather, the party has spilled out from the veranda onto the back lawn, the women in summer dresses, the men sporting blazers whose brass buttons catch the late-afternoon sun, and our route takes us right through them. I think I can impersonate a caddy—I *am* a caddy—but can Jerzy project the body language and entitlement of a brat? And will his weight and bad skin work against him? Surely one of the members will notice something amiss in our bearing or breeding and see us for the interlopers we are.

Among those directly in our path is a middle-aged man who looks strikingly familiar. That's not surprising. Augusta's roster is loaded with captains of industry, so perhaps I've seen his face staring back at me from the magazine rack at the dentist or the jacket of a bestseller. But I've been avoiding the dentist for months and haven't read anything except the sports section in years, and I know I've seen this face recently.

Then it all falls into place like that last piece of fruit in a slot machine window. He was the guy sitting next to Nantz in the Butler Cabin, the one who asked Tiger to please place the green jacket on his good friend and new Masters champion, Mark O'Meara. It's Hootie fucking Johnson, chairman of Augusta National, and at the same moment that I recognize him, Hootie reaches out his hand and claps it down on Jerzy's shoulder.

58

"What's your name, son?"

"Brune, sir. It's a pleasure to make your acquaintance."

"Then call me Hootie, for Christ's sake! How was it out there?"

"Hootie, it was awesome," says Jerzy, the last bit of left-over accent cutting through the molasses of Hootie's drawl. "I don't think I've ever seen the course in better condition. It's so good we're heading back out for another nine."

"Got to make hay while the sun shines. After all, you never know when you're going to get down here again."

"Sad but true, Hootie."

"Your home course?" asks Johnson. Since his right hand is still on Jerzy's shoulder, he refers to the Big Oaks cap with his gin and tonic.

"Correct," says Jerzy, after a slight delay. "Just outside Chicago."

"Why haven't I heard of it?"

"It's still a bit under the radar," says Jerzy, his voice dipping to a whisper. "But not for long, I fear. The next time you're in the vicinity, I'd be honored to give you a tour."

As impressed as I am with Jerzy's performance, astounded even, I'm more than ready for this delightful exchange to be over. I know Jerzy's wardrobe is right, but under such prolonged exposure something is bound to out him, whether it's the accent or the mysterious *home course*. Even after Hootie finally takes his hand off Jerzy's shoulder, the conversational ball keeps going back and forth.

"I just might take you up on that, young man. What's your last name, Brune?"

"Pickering."

"Pickering," repeats Hootie softly to himself. "Brune Pickering?" Then he turns to me. "And how about you? I don't believe we've met either."

"Rudy, sir. Rudy Laplante. I started this week."

"Rudy Laplante? You don't say?"

"Yes, sir."

"Well, Brune, how's old Rudy doing?"

"Very well. And he's not as old as he looks. I believe Rudy has the makings of a first-rate caddy, and you can quote me on that."

"He's got the Brune seal of approval, does he?"

"Correct. Of course, there's been a misread now and then, and a missed club here and there, but not even Hogan always got the wind right at Golden Bell."

"Fair point, Brune."

For a few seconds that seem like a month, Hootie stares at each of us in turn; then he shakes his head and chuckles softly to himself. "Well. I'll let you both get to it, then. Hit 'em straight."

"Thanks, Hootie. I'm so pleased I finally got a chance to meet you."

"Me too, Brune."

When Hootie repairs to the veranda, Jerzy and I continue to the first tee, which, without hundreds of patrons surrounding it, seems oddly naked. "Jerzy, you have any idea who that man was?"

"No idea."

"Me neither."

59

LESS THAN THREE WEEKS ago, sitting in my den with Louie, I watched Sam Snead walk onto the first tee and hit the ceremonial first shot of the '98 Masters. Now I'm watching Jerzy Solarski, a seventeen-year-old from Bucharest, who three months ago knocked on my door with a shovel, tee it up from the same spot. Almost as unlikely, I've now spent two hours on a course where I've fantasized playing for forty years, haven't taken a single swing, and don't seem to mind.

With Hootie and company sipping their second or third cocktails, Jerzy and I have Prosper Berckmans's former nursery entirely to ourselves. You could argue that the experience is more rarefied than actually playing the Masters, where you're obliged to share it with the likes of Tiger and Phil, a hundred other pros, and tens of thousands of fans, I mean *patrons*.

Aside from those snippets of an old-timer stooping over on the first tee on Thursday nights on ESPN, the front side is untelevised, and that makes playing Tea Olive, Pink Dogwood, Flowering Peach, and Flowering Crab Apple a lot different than playing Camellia, White Dogwood, and Golden Bell. From our shared reading, Jerzy and I know the approximate layouts, but we haven't witnessed golf history on every hole. That takes the edge off considerably, and as the sun begins its swift descent, Jerzy pars two of them and the par/bogey train keeps chugging through the Georgia pines.

As we walk off 5, Magnolia, the sun dips beneath the trees, and now the birds stop chirping. Engulfed in quiet, it's harder to ignore the question I've been dodging all day, if not all week, which, of course, is "Why?" Why are we doing this? What message am I trying to convey? What, if anything, am I hoping to instill in an impressionable young mind beyond a healthy disrespect for private property and a love for destination trespassing?

Well, here's my answer. To have some fun in this life and avoid swallowing a mouthful of shit per day takes more than luck, and this is a lesson, however ill-conceived, in audacity. If the last year or so has taught me anything, it's that every once in a while you need to take a deep breath, do your best impersonation of a badass, and see where it goes. If nothing else, you might make some new friends as interesting as Earl, Stump, and Jerzy, and what's more precious than that?

On the famous back nine, we felt like a couple of tourists gawking at golf's Eiffel Tower. Finally, we can just play. Hit it. Find it. And hit it again. Do that, good things tend to happen, even to mediocre golfers. Over the next three holes, Jerzy cards two more pars, and when he slides in a six-footer on 8 for the second one, the laid-back quality of our afternoon evaporates. Suddenly, I'm as nervous as I was walking beside Earl up the 18th fairway at Shoal Creek on Sunday.

60

"YOU KNOW WHERE WE are right now?" asks Jerzy.

"Number nine," I say, "Carolina Cherry. Golf course called Augusta National."

"In addition to that?"

"Eight over," I concede.

"Correct. So I need to birdie one of the next two."

"Yup."

If my share of the dialogue seems flat, it's intentional. I appreciate the weight of the moment, at least as much as Jerzy, but I'm doing my best to pretend otherwise. After sixteen holes, Jerzy has eight pars and eight bogeys. Since Augusta National is a par 72, that means he's sitting on 80, and if he can play the next two holes in 1-under-par, he'll shoot 79.

For every hacker who's ever teed it up in vain, breaking 80 is the Promised Land, and getting there for the first time is like meeting Saint Peter at the pearly gate. In terms of personal significance, it trumps playing Augusta National, Pebble Beach, and St. Andrews combined. It isn't even close. Let's say that on the same day that you eked out an 83 at Augusta National, you drove to a muni on the wrong side of town and shot 79, "no gimmes, no mulligans, no bullshit," to break 80 for the first time. Which round at which course do you think you'll be replaying in your mind all night? I'll give you a clue. It's not the one with the azaleas.

On the other hand, if you're going to break 80 for the first time, Augusta National is a highly auspicious place to do it. In order of magnitude, it would be like losing your virginity to Marilyn Monroe. And having a signed document, suitable for framing, to verify it. People have gone on to become president for a lot less.

Unfortunately, Jerzy's chances of doing one are about as good as the other, and Marilyn, bless her generous soul, has been dead thirty-six years. The problem is the difficulty of our remaining two holes. The 9th, with its signature three-tier green, is one of the hardest on the front nine, and the 10th, a 495-yard par 4, is the hardest hole on the course. The last two holes are so long and tough that playing them even would constitute a minor miracle, but as I guess you know, the name of this book is not *The Minor Miracle at Augusta.*

"So how am I going to get this done?" asks Jerzy.

"Birdieing nine would be a good start."

61

JERZY AND I STAND on the 9th tee and squint at what's left of the fairway. There's so little light, the only way to get an idea what we're facing is to pull out the yardage book. With Jerzy squinting over my shoulder at the diagram, I lay out the challenge. Since we both know he needs birdie, I don't sugarcoat it.

"Carolina Cherry is a dogleg left. Downhill off the tee, uphill to the green. It's all about the tee shot. If you can get it to the bottom of the hill, where you can hit a short iron or even a wedge on your second, you've got a much better chance for birdie. To do that, you need to get all of it, and it's got to be straight, because there are trees on both sides."

Jerzy's tee shot—a low hard top—is on me. Tell a seventeen-year-old, or even a nearly fifty-two-year-old, he needs a big drive, he's going to overswing every time, and despite the lousy light, I know it's nowhere near the bottom of the hill. As we soon discover, it hasn't even rolled off the top plateau, and when I step off the distance to the nearest sprinkler head and do the math, I get 221 to the center of the green.

There's just enough light to make out the flag on the left side, and by referring to the yardage book, I determine that it's cut in the second of the three tiers. When I also see that the green tilts sharply from back to front and, to a lesser degree, from left to right, I can't resist a dark smile. The only shot with a chance in hell to stay on that second tier, where he would have a realistic putt at birdie, is the one I practiced all winter at Big Oaks. And he's got to hit it, not me.

"You're in luck," I say. "This calls for a high draw, and I'm something of an expert on this shot. We could spend a month on it, but here's the fifteen-second tutorial: move the ball back closer to your right foot, close your stance, and think about hitting the inside of the ball."

I feel like a quarterback sketching a play in the dirt on the last drive of the Super Bowl, but I'm not Bart Starr and Jerzy's not Paul Hornung. Or maybe he is, because in his first attempt, with 79 on the line, he hits it purer than I did all winter with nothing at stake, and before the ball disappears from sight, we can see it bend gently toward the flag.

"Congratulations, Jerzy. According to your new friend Earl Fielder, you just hit the suavest shot in golf."

"Who am I to contradict Earl?" says Jerzy.

Now all that's left is the minor technicality of that pesky twenty-two-footer. Jerzy steps up to it as if it holds all the peril of a tap-in and rolls it dead center. Let's see what he's like in thirty years after he's missed a mile of five-footers.

62

"Jerzy, that was sweet. Now all you got left is the hard part—making a four on ten."

Somewhere between the 9th green and the 10th tee, the last bit of light drains from the sky. If this were a tournament, they'd have sounded the horn thirty minutes ago. At least we're on the back nine again, and along with Owl's trusty yardage book, we have the benefit of having seen this hole in Central Time on CBS.

"Another downhill dogleg left," says Jerzy, squinting at the diagram. "Looks like nine."

"Particularly in the dark," I say. "This one is forty yards longer, but there's a speed slot on the left side of the fairway. If you can drop it in there, it plays about the same. Take a three-wood, put an easy swing on it, and let the slope and gravity do the rest."

As a preamble, it's a helluva lot better than what I came

up with on 9. Jerzy strikes it solid, gets the sought-after roll, and when we find it just off the left side of the fairway, 185 yards from the center of the green, this absurd pipe dream still seems possible. From here, the green is harder to see than the flag, but by working off the sand on the right and the yardage book, I place the flag back and left.

"You've got one ninety-three to the pin," I say. "It's cooler now, so it's going to play all that. Aim for the right side of the green and don't worry about the bunker. It's much better than being left."

I hand him the 4-iron, and Jerzy delivers his third pure swing in a row, like he's just getting warmed up. In fact, it's too good, or maybe he catches a flier, or more likely I gave him the wrong club, because he airmails the green. After it soars over the trap, it disappears from view, and as we tilt forward and strain our ears in that direction, we hear it hit a branch and then another and maybe even a third.

Just like Shoal Creek all over again, I think as the pines play pinball with Jerzy's 79. Last hole. Last swing. All we need is par, and I pull the wrong stick. Funny thing about golf acoustics—sometimes a ball hitting a tree sounds exactly like a ball splashing into a pond.

63

WITH THE RESILIENCE OF youth, Jerzy bounds after it.

"Jerzy, wait up. I got to make you hit a provisional. In this light, we might never find that ball."

Even if we don't, and Jerzy limps home with a triple, he still shoots 82, and the last thing I want to do when this is over is hand him a scorecard with a big fat asterisk attached. Whatever he shoots today is going to be legit. No gimmes. No mulligans. No bullshit.

I hand him the 5, and he goes through the same routine he did with the 4—a practice swing, a waggle, and go. Again he hits it well, and when we get closer, we see that it's rolled onto the front edge. Then we head to the spot beyond the right trap where his first ball disappeared.

In the trees, it's three shades darker, and a glance at my watch shows we're coming up on our appointed rendezvous with Earl and Stump. By now it's a cool Georgia night—all pretense of a late afternoon or early evening is gone—and we spend the next few minutes weaving through the pine straw trying to will a Titleist into view. When that doesn't happen in five minutes, I call off the search and we return to the green.

"All that means," I say, "is that you're going to have to make one last putt. The goal was to get you on the green with a putt for par, and we've done that. Whether his name is Ben Crenshaw or Dave Stockton, there is no one I'd rather see putt this ball than you."

I don't know what makes the putt harder—the distance or the darkness. Between the ball and the flag are over a hundred feet of barely visible green, and a big break from right to left. I wish I could be more specific, but in this light, I can't. The only thing in our favor is that it's uphill.

I know that in the course of this tale, I've pushed your credulity to the limit. If I tell you Jerzy drains a 110-foot putt with about 20 feet of break in total darkness on the hardest hole at Augusta National to break 80 for the first time, will that be a bridge too far? In any case, all I can do is tell you what happened.

After we've learned all that we can by studying an invisible green, I send Jerzy down to his ball with his magic putter and I head to the hole to tend the flag. At the bottom of the green, Jerzy is a dark shape, and behind him at the top of the hill, the light in the Crow's Nest looks like a low moon. "Don't be afraid to hit it. The one thing you can't do is leave it short."

On opposite ends of the green, Jerzy takes his practice strokes and I reach for the pin. I've already made one gaffe on this hole. I don't want to compound it by getting the flag stuck and then yanking so hard that the entire cup comes out with it. To ensure that the flag will slide out smoothly, I twist it back and forth, and something rattles at my feet. When I look down, I see a white Titleist with a blue *J* and *S* on each side of the 3.

"Don't putt it, Jerzy," I manage to shout in time. "Pick it up. Your first ball is in the hole. You didn't just break eighty. You broke seventy-eight."

Here's the final scorecard after I pencil in his 2 on Camellia. No matter how many times you add it up, it comes to 77.

Hole	Par	Jerzy		HOLE	PAR	Jerzy	
1	4	5		10	4	2 ℓ	
2	5	⑤		11	4	④	
3	4	5		12	3	4	
4	3	③		13	5	⑤	
5	4	5		14	4	5	
6	3	③		15	5'	6	
7	4	5		16	3	③	
8	5	⑤		17	4	5	
9	4	3 6		18	4	④	
Out	36	39		TOTAL	72	77	

SCORER: *Travis McKinley* ATTEST: _____   DATE: *April 25th*

64

"How does it feel?" I ask when Jerzy finally reaches the hole and sees the evidence for himself.

"Ridiculous good," he says. He plucks the ball from the hole and holds it in the moonlight. "So ridiculous good, it should be illegal."

"Actually, it is."

"Well, fuck 'em if they can't take a joke."

"That's what I say."

We give ourselves a minute before we vacate the green. Then we walk past the 11th tee, where our round began, and for the first time today, a part of Augusta National is familiar, not because we've seen it countless times on television but because we stood on this very spot three hours before, and that makes for a richer strain of nostalgia.

The feeling of déjà vu is even stronger as we head up the 11th fairway, crest the hill, and gaze out toward the amoeba-shaped shadows that are the 11th and 12th greens. Now the moon is all the way up and crickets have replaced the birds, and as we walk through the dew-drenched grass, I feel the same elation I did as a twelve-year-old, when after *"two more holes"* and *"just one more"* and then *"one more and that's it,"* I raced back through the sudden nightfall toward the Creekview parking lot.

Fifty yards short of the green, I hear Rae's Creek, and then I smell it. We step out of our shoes and socks and wade back across. On the other side, I lay Jerzy's bag on the ground and, from our dry perch on his clubs, stare back across the creek at Amen Corner.

"Jerzy, you know what was your best swing all day?"

Jerzy shrugs, still hauling aboard his birdie/eagle finish.

"The only one that didn't count. After you knocked it into the trees on ten, you stepped up to the provisional with the exact same attitude as the first. That showed a lot of heart. I'm really proud of you for that. There are a lot of pros who couldn't have done that. In fact, you're sitting next to one of them."

"That's because you're a great big baby."

"Correct."

After one last glance across the creek, we turn our backs on Augusta National and make the slow climb through the pines. I should have thought to pack a flashlight, because scrambling over the wall is borderline dangerous, particularly for an exhausted almost fifty-two-year-old. Once we're back on legal ground, Jerzy finds the spot where I stashed my clubs, and we slip through the trees onto the grounds of the Augusta Country Club.

"You think Hootie is going to take you up on that tour?"

"I hope so," says Jerzy. "When I said I'd be honored to show him around Big Oaks, I meant it. It's still my favorite place. Always will be. That reminds me, there's something I've really got to say."

"What?"

"Next time, I'm caddying."

"No shit."

For a couple of minutes, we stand in the dark and smile, savoring a ridiculous good day. Then Earl turns on a flashlight and we see the two carts parked side by side.

"Well?" asks Stump. "How'd our boy do?"

"That's it?" I ask. "No hello? It's good to see you? We were a little worried about you guys? None of that? Just, what did he shoot?"

"That bad, huh?"

"Afraid so," I say. "Seventy-seven…from the tips."

Stump emits a sound only a 220-pound tobacco-chewing redneck is capable of producing without injury. "This calls for a celebration, and I know just the place. But Jerzy's going to need ID."

"For fuck's sake, Stump," says Earl. "After everything they've done today, I think they're capable of getting themselves into your silly-ass bar."

"They better be. Because Wednesday is karaoke night."

Stump motions for Jerzy to take the seat next to him and I get in the cart with Earl and we race beneath the moon to the empty parking lot. The last thing I hear, before their cart slips out of earshot, is Stump telling Jerzy, "You got a nice little game, son, keep it up."

Epilogue

IT'S A LITTLE MORE than two months later, and I'm sitting in the den with Sarah, Noah, and Louie, watching golf on television. For obvious reasons, I've been doing more spectating than competing this summer, and this weekend is particularly rough because it's the U.S. Senior Open, my one shining moment as a pro. That must be why Sarah, who wouldn't normally spend Saturday indoors, has joined me and Noah on the couch.

The good news is that both Earl and Stump are having a great Open. Not only are they tied for third at four under par, they're paired in the second-to-last group, and with Lee Trevino rounding out the threesome, they're guaranteed plenty of airtime. In fact, the broadcast opens with Stump, shameless as ever, waving his cap back and forth and whipping the crowd into a frenzy. When he finally puts the cap back on his head, I can't make out the name on the front, but I can tell it's not Titleist or Skoal, his primary sponsors.

"Noah, can you read what it says on Stump's hat?"

"State," says Noah.

"Must be Georgia State," I say. "Either that, or he signed a new deal with an insurance company."

When Trevino takes the tee, the crowd is even more raucous, and when he doffs his cap, I notice the same unfamiliar white font.

"How about Lee's hat?" I ask Noah. "Can you read that?"

"*Re* something," he says.

Next and last is Earl, and as he goes into his brisk preshot routine, I see he's wearing the same boxy black hat with the same simple white font on the crown, this time a word beginning with *M*.

"Your name is on his hat," says Sarah, stunned. "It says McKinley."

"It does, Dad."

Earl splits the fairway for the millionth time, and after his ball stops rolling, Earl, Stump, and Trevino pose side by side, their hats reading: MCKINLEY, STATE, RE-IN. Then Earl switches places with Lee, and the three hats read: RE-IN STATE MCKINLEY.

The three are still side by side on the tee box and beaming into the camera when my favorite on-course interviewer, Dave Marr, hustles over and asks, "What's with the hats, gentlemen?" and shoves a microphone in front of Earl's face.

"This is for our buddy Travis McKinley," says Earl, "who got suspended for nothing more than a scuffle between consenting adults. He's been out four months now, and that's four months too long."

"Enough is enough," says Stump.

"And how about you, Lee? You feel the same way?"

"These guys were both there. If they think it's ridiculous, that's good enough for me. Besides, Travis is one of my favorite players. I miss him, and I'm sure the fans do, too."

"Dad, can you believe Trevino just called you one of his favorite players?"

"No, I can't...and it's too late to tape it."

It doesn't stop there. On the second tee, Earl's Platoon takes up the chant: "Reinstate McKinley...Reinstate McKinley!" and when they tire of that, switch to the catchier "It can't wait! Reinstate!" often with Stump out front conducting the choir. Earl and Stump must have been plotting this for weeks, because by the back nine, half the field has switched to a black cap with either RE-IN, STATE, or MCKINLEY on it. I don't have to look over at Sarah to know that tears are streaming down her face, but I risk it anyway.

Overwhelmed, I retreat to the backyard with Louie, sip my beer on a lawn chair, and gaze up at the trees. Sarah and I have lived in this house nearly thirty years, and the branches get fuller and lovelier each summer, and for twenty minutes I watch and listen as the leaves move in the gentle breeze. When my cell phone goes off and I see the call is from Ponte Vedra, Florida, I consider not answering, but on the fifth ring I succumb.

"Travis, it's Tim Finchem."

"I had no idea they were planning this. Are you calling because you want me to ask them to stop?"

"No, it's too late for that. I'm calling to eat crow. If your fellow players want you back, who am I to stand in the way? As of this moment, your suspension is officially suspended. You are once again a member in full standing on the Senior Tour."

I hear the words, but they're more than I can absorb, so I close my eyes and listen to the leaves.

"Travis, you there?"

"Yes, Commissioner. Thanks very much."

"Don't thank me, Travis. Thank Earl and Stump and Lee. You got a lot of good friends out here. I hope you know that.... One other thing, before I forget. A couple of weeks ago, I got a call from Hootie Johnson. You know Hootie, right? The chairman of Augusta National?"

"I know who he is. I can't say I know him."

"Well, apparently he knows you. I don't know what prompted this, and I'm not sure I want to, but he said if you ever want to play Augusta National you should give him a call. Good night, Travis, and welcome back."

I stare at the rustling leaves for another hour before I go back inside and share the news.

Winner of the Edgar™ Award for
Best First Novel

THE
THOMAS BERRYMAN
NUMBER

For an excerpt, turn the page

PART I

THE FIRST TRIP NORTH

WEST HAMPTON, JULY 9

IN NINETEEN SIXTY-NINE I won a George Polk prize for some life-style articles about black Mayor Jimmie Lee Horn of Nashville. The series was called "A Walker's Guide to Shanty-town," but it ran in the *Citizen-Reporter* as "Black Lives."

It wasn't a bad writing job, but it was more a case of being in the right place at the right time: I'd written life-affirming stories about a black man in Tennessee, just a year after Martin Luther King had died there.

It felt right to people who judged things somewhere. They said the series was "vital."

So I was lucky in '69.

I figured things were beginning to even out the day I drove into the William Pound Institute in West Hampton, Long Island. On account of my assignment there I wouldn't be writing any of the article about Horn's murder. The good Horn assignments had already gone elsewhere. Higher up.

I parked my rent-a-car in a crowded yard marked ALL HOSPITAL VISITORS. Then, armed with tape recorder, suit-coat over my arm too, I made my way along a broken flag-stone path tunneling through bent old oak trees.

I didn't really notice a lot about the hospital at first. I was busy feeling sorry for myself.

Random Observation: The man looking most obviously lost and disturbed at the William Pound Institute—baggy white suit, torn panama hat, Monkey Ward dress shirt—must have been me.

Here was Ochs Jones, thirty-one-year-old cornpone sa-vant, never before having been north of Washington D.C.

But the Brooks Brothers doctors, the nurses, the fire-haired patients walking around the hospital paid no atten-tion.

Which isn't easy—even at 9:30 on a drizzly, unfriendly morning.

Generally I'm noticed most places.

My blond hair is close-cropped, just a little seedy on the sides, already falling out on top—so that my head resem-bles a Franciscan monk's. I'm slightly cross-eyed without my glasses (and because of the rain I had them off). Moreover, I'm 6'7", and I stand out quite nicely without the aid of quirky clothes.

No one noticed, though. One doctory-looking woman said, "Hello, Michael." "Ochs," I told her. That was about it for introductions.

Less than 1% believing Ben Toy might have a story for me, I dutifully followed all the blue-arrowed signs marked BOWDITCH.

The grounds of the Pound Institute were clean and fresh-smelling and green as a state park. The hospital reminded me of an eastern university campus, someplace with a name like Ithaca, or Swarthmore, or Hobart.

It was nearly ten as I walked past huge red-brick houses along an equally red cobblestone road.

Occasionally a Cadillac or Mercedes crept by at the posted ten m.p.h. speed limit.

The federalist-style houses I passed were the different wards of the hospital.

One was for the elderly bedridden. Another was for the elderly who could still putter around—predominantly lobotomies.

One four-story building housed nothing but children aged over ten years. A little girl sat rocking in the window of one of the downstairs rooms. She reminded me of Anthony Perkins at the end of *Psycho*.

I jotted down a few observations and felt silly making them. I kept one wandering eye peeled for Ben Toy's ward: Bowditch: male maximum security.

A curious thing happened to me in front of the ward for young girls.

A round-shouldered girl was sitting on the wet front lawn close to the road where I was walking. She was playing a blond-wood guitar and singing *Ballad of a Thin Man*, the Bob Dylan song, just about talking the lyrics.

I was Ochs Jones, thirty-one, father of two daughters . . . The only violent act I could recall in my life, was *hearing*—as a boy—that my great-uncle Ochs Jones had been hanged in Moon, Kentucky, as a horsethief . . . and *no*, I didn't know what was going on.

As a matter of fact, I knew considerably less than I thought I did.

The last of the Federal-style houses was more rambling, less formal and kept-up than any of the others: It bordered on scrub pine woods with very green waist-high underbrush running through it. A high stockade fence had been built up as the ward's backyard.

BOWDITCH a fancy gold plaque by the front door said.

The man who'd contacted the *Citizen-Reporter*, Dr. Alan Shulman, met me on the front porch. Right off, Shulman informed me that this was an unusual and delicate situation for him. The hospital, he said, had only divulged information about patients a few times before—and that invariably had to do with court cases. "But an assassination," he said, "is somewhat extraordinary. We *want* to help."

Shulman was very New Yorkerish, with curly, scraggly black hair. He wore the kind of black-frame eyeglasses with little silver arrows in the corners. He was probably in his mid-thirties, with some kind of Brooklyn or Queens accent that was odd to my ear.

Some men slouching inside behind steel-screened windows seemed to be finding us quite a curious combination to observe.

A steady flow of collected rainwater rattled the drainpipe on the porch.

It made it a little harder for Shulman and myself to hear one another's side of the argument that was developing.

"I left my home around five, five-fifteen this morning," I said in a quick, agitated bluegrass drawl.

"I took an awful Southern Airways flight up to Kennedy Airport...awful flight...stopped at places like Dohren, Alabama...Then I drove an Econo-Car out to God-knows-where-but-I-don't, Long Island. And now, you're not going to let me in to see Toy...Is that right Doctor Shulman? That's right, isn't it?"

Shulman just nodded the curly black head.

Then he said something like this to me: "Ben Toy had a very bad, piss-poor night last night. He's been up and down since he got in here...I think he *wants* to get better now...I don't think he wants to kill himself right now...So maybe you can talk with him tomorrow. Maybe even tonight. Not now, though."

"Aw shit," I shook my head. I loosened up my tie and a laugh snorted out through my nose. The laugh is a big flaw in my business style. I can't really take myself too seriously, and it shows.

When Shulman laughed too I started to like him. He had a good way of laughing that was hard to stay pissed off at. I imagined he used it on all his patients.

"Well, at least invite me in for some damn coffee," I grinned.

The doctor took me into a back door through Bowditch's nurse's station.

I caught a glimpse of nurses, some patients, and a lot of Plexiglas surrounding the station. We entered another room, a wood-paneled conference room, and Shulman personally mixed me some Sanka.

After some general small talk, he told me why he'd started to feel that Ben Toy was somehow involved in the murders of Jimmie Horn, Bert Poole, and Lieutenant Mart Weesner.

I told him why most of the people at the *Citizen* doubted it.

Our reasons had to do with motion pictures of the Horn shooting. The films clearly showed young Poole shooting Horn in the chest and face.

Alan Shulman's reasons had to do with gut feelings. (And also with the nagging fact that the police would probably never remove Ben Toy from an institution to face trial.)

Like the man or not, I was not overly impressed with his theories.

"Don't you worry," he assured me, "this story will be worth your time and air fare . . . if you handle it right."

As part of the idea of getting my money's worth out of the trip, I drove about six miles south after leaving the hospital.

I slipped into a pair of cut-offs in my rent-a-car, then went for my first swim in an ocean.

If I'd known how little time I'd be having for the next five months, I would have squeezed even more out of the free afternoon.

The rainy day turned into beautiful, pink-and-blue-skied night.

I was wearing blue jeans and white shirttails, walking down the hospital's cobblestone road again. It was 8:30 that same evening and I'd been asked to come back to Bowditch.

A bear-bearded, rabbinical-looking attendant was assigned to record and supervise my visit with Ben Toy. A ring of keys and metal badges jangled from the rope belt around his Levi's. A plastic name pin said that he was MR. RONALD ASHER, SENIOR MENTAL HEALTH WORKER.

The two of us, both carrying pads and pencils, walked down a long, gray-carpeted hall with airy, white-curtained bedrooms on either side.

Something about being locked in the hall made me a little tense. I was combing my hair with my fingers as I walked along.

"Our quiet room's about the size of a den," Asher told me.

"It's a seclusion room. Seclusion room's used for patients who act-out violently. Act-out against the staff, or other patients, or against themselves."

"Which did Ben Toy do?" I asked the attendant.

"Oh shit." Big white teeth showed in his beard. "He's been in there for all three at one time or another. He can be a total jerk-off, and then again he can be a pretty nice guy."

Asher stopped in front of the one closed door in the hallway. While he opened it with two different keys, I looked inside through a book-sized observation window.

The room *was* tiny.

It had gunboat metal screens and red bars on small, mud-spattered windows. A half-eaten bowl of cereal and milk was on the windowsill. Outside was the stockade wall and an exercise yard.

Ben Toy was seated on the room's only furniture, a narrow blue pinstriped mattress. He was wearing a black cowboy Stetson, but when he saw my face in the window he took it off.

"Come on the hell in," I heard a friendly, muffled voice. "The door's only triple-locked."

Just then Asher opened it.

Ben Toy was a tall, thin man, about thirty, with a fast, easy, hustler's smile. His blond hair was oily, unwashed. He was Jon Voight on the skids.

Toy was wearing white pajama bottoms with no top. His ribs were sticking out to be counted. His chest was covered with curly, auburn hair, however, and he was basically rugged-looking.

According to Asher, Toy had tried to starve himself when he'd first come in the hospital. Asher said he'd been burly back then.

When Toy spoke his voice was soft. He seemed to be trying to sound hip. N.Y.-L.A. dope world sounds.

"You look like a Christian monk, man," he drawled pleasantly.

"No shit," I laughed, and he laughed too. He seemed pretty normal. Either that, or the black-bearded aide was a snake charmer.

After a little bit of measuring each other up, Toy and I went right into Jimmie Horn.

Actually, I started on the subject, but Toy did most of the talking.

He knew what Horn looked like; where Horn had lived; precisely where his campaign headquarters had been. He knew the names of Jimmie Horn's two children; his parents' names; all sorts of impossible trivia nobody outside of Tennessee would have any interest in.

At that point, I found myself talking rapidly and listening very closely. The Sony was burning up tape.

"You think you know who shot Horn up?" Toy said to me.

"I think I do, yes. A man named Bert Poole shot him. A chronic bumbler who lived in Nashville all his life. A fuck-up."

"This *bumbler*," Toy asked. "How did you figure out he did it?"

His question was very serious; forensic, in a country pool hall way. He was slowly turning the black Stetson around on his fist.

"For one thing," I said, "I saw it on television. For another thing, I've talked to a shitload of people who were there."

Toy frowned at me. "Guess you talked to the wrong shitload of people," he said. He was acting very sure of himself.

It was just after that when Toy spoke of the contact, or bagman, involved with Jimmie Horn.

It was then also that I heard the name Thomas Berryman for the first time.

PROVINCETOWN, JUNE 6

The time Toy spoke of was early June of that year; the place was Provincetown, Massachusetts.

Young Harley John Wynn parked in the shadows behind the Provincetown City Hall and started off toward Commercial Street with visions of power and money dancing in his head. Wynn was handsome, fair and baby-faced like the early F. Scott Fitzgerald photographs. His car was a Lincoln Mark IV. In some ways he was like Thomas Berryman. Both men were thoroughly modern, coldly sober, distressingly sure of themselves.

For over three weeks, Harley Wynn had been making enquiries about Berryman. He'd finally been contacted the Tuesday before that weekend.

The meeting had been set up for Provincetown. Wynn was asked to be reading a *Boston Globe* on one of the benches in front of the City Hall at 9:45 p.m.

*   *   *

It was almost 9:30, and cool, even for Cape Cod in June.

The grass was freshly mown, and it had a good smell for Wynn: it reminded him of college quadrangles in the deep South. Cape Cod itself reminded him of poliomyelitis.

Careful of his shoeshine, he stayed in tree shadows just off the edge of the lawn. He sidestepped a snake, which turned out to be a tangle of electrician's tape.

He was startled by some green willow fingers, and realized he was still in a driving fog.

It wasn't night on Commercial Street, and as Wynn came into the amber lights he began to smell light cologne instead of sod.

He sat on one of the freshly painted benches—bone white, like the City Hall—and he saw that he was among male and female homosexuals.

There were several tall blonds in scarlet and powder blue halter suits. Small, bushy-haired men in white bucks and thongs, and bright sailor-style pants. There were tank-shirts and flapping sandals and New York *Times* magazine models posing under street-lamps.

Wynn lighted a Marlboro, noticed uneasiness in his big hands, and took a long, deep breath.

He looked up and down the street for Ben Toy.

Up on the porch of the City Hall, his eyes stopped to watch flour-white gargoyles and witchy teenagers parading to and from the public toilets.

Harley Wynn's hand kept slipping inside his suitjacket and touching a thick, brown envelope.

Across the street, Ben Toy, thirty, and Thomas Berryman, twenty-nine, were sitting together drinking beer and Taylor Cream in a rear alcove of the A. J. Fogarty bar.

Rough-hewn men with expensive sunglasses, they brought to mind tennis bums.

They were talking about Texas with two Irish girls they'd discovered in Hyannis. One girl wore a tartan skirt and top; the other was wearing a pea-coat, rolled-up jeans, and striped baseball-player socks.

Toy and Berryman told old Texas stories back and forth, and listened to less-polished but promising Boston tales.

Oona, the taller, prettier girl, was telling how she some-times walked Massachusetts Avenue in Boston, pretending she was a paraplegic. "Like all these business types from the Pru," she said, "they get too embarrassed to ogle. I can be by myself if I want to."

Thomas Berryman stared at her boozily with great red eyes. "That's a very funny bit," he smiled slightly. Then he was tilting his head back and forth with the pendulum of a Miller beer clock.

It was ten o'clock. Miller's was still the champagne of bot-tled beers. Bette Midler was singing boogie on the jukebox.

A handsome blond man was talking to Oona from a stool at the bar. "You know who you remind me of," he smiled brightly, "you remind me of Lauren Hutton."

"Excuse me," the tall girl smiled back innocently, "but you've obviously mistaken me for someone who gives a shit."

This time Berryman laughed out loud. All of them did.

Then Berryman spoke quietly to Ben Toy. "Don't you think he's been waiting long enough now?"

Toy licked beer foam off his upper lip. "No," he said. "Hell no."

"You're sure about that, Ben? Got it buttoned up for me?..."

"The man's just getting uncomfortable about now. Taking an occasional deep breath. Getting real p.o.'d at me. I want him good and squirmy when I go talk to him ...Besides though, I don't need this paranoia shit."

Berryman grinned at him. "Just checking," he said. "So long as you deliver, you do it any way you want to."

At 10:30, forty-five minutes after the arranged time, Ben Toy got up and slowly walked up to A. J. Fogarty's front window.

He was later to remember watching Wynn through the Calligraphia window lettering. Wynn in an expensive blue suit with gray pinstripes. Wynn in brown Florsheim tie shoes and a matching brown belt. Southern macho, Toy thought.

For his part, Ben Toy was wearing a blue muslin shirt with a red butterfly design on the back. With pearl snaps. He was a big, blue-eyed man; Berryman's back-up; Berryman's old friend from Texas; a Texas rake.

Among boys in Amarillo, Ben Toy had once been known as "the funniest man in America."

He smiled now as Wynn started to read the *Boston Globe* again. The money was apparently in his left side jacket pocket. He kept rubbing his elbow up against it.

Harley John Wynn couldn't have helped noticing Toy as he left Fogarty's bar. Toy looked like a drunken lord: he had long blond hair, and an untroubled face.

He walked slowly behind a college boy in a mauve Boston College sweatshirt. He waded through various kinds of Volkswagens on the street; then he calmly sat down on Harley Wynn's bench.

In his own right, southern lawyer Harley Wynn was a cool, collected, and moderately successful young man. He knew himself to be clearheaded and analytical. He identified with men like Bernie Cornfeld and Robert Yablans—the brash, bootleg quarterback types in the business world. Now he was making a big play of his own.

Wynn's generally *together* appearance didn't fool Ben Toy, however. The southern man's hands had given him away. They were sweaty, and had taken newspaper print up off the *Boston Globe*. Telltale smudges were on his forehead and right on the tip of his nose.

"I was just thinking about all of this," Wynn gestured around the street and environs. "The fact that you're nearly an hour late. The faggots ... You're trying very hard to put me at a disadvantage." The southerner smiled boyishly. He held out an athletic-looking hand. "I approve of that," he said.

Ben Toy ignored the outstretched hand. He grunted indifferently and looked down at his boottips.

Harley Wynn laughed at the way nervous men try to condescend.

Toy still said nothing.

"All right then," Wynn's southern twang stiffened. "...Horn's a fairly intelligent nigger ...Very intelligent, matter of fact."

Toy looked up and established eye contact with the man.

"Horn has affronted sensibilities in the South, however. That's neither here nor there. My interest in the matter, your interest, is purely monetary." He looked for some nod of agreement from Ben Toy.

"I don't have anything to say to that," Toy finally spoke. He lighted a cigarette, spread his long, blue-jeaned legs, sat back on the bench and watched traffic.

The young lawyer began to force smiles. He was capable of getting quick acceptance and he was overly used to it. He glanced to where Toy was looking, expecting someone else to join them.

"You'll be provided with detailed information on Horn," he said. "Daily routines and schedules if you like …" The lawyer spewed out information like a computer.

"All right, stop it now." Toy finally swung around and looked at Wynn again. His teeth were clenched tight.

He jabbed the man in the stomach with his fist. "I could kill you, man," he said. "Stop fucking around with me."

The lawyer was pale, perspiring at the hairline. He wasn't comprehending.

Toy cleared his throat before he spoke again. He spit up an impressive gob on the lawn. Headlights went across Harley Wynn's eyes, then over his own.

"Berryman wants a reason," he said. "He wants to know exactly why you're offering all this money."

Toy cautioned Harley Wynn with his finger before he let him answer. "Don't fuck with me."

"I haven't been fucking with you," Wynn said. "I understand the seriousness of this. The precautions ... In fact, that's the explanation you want ... There can be no suspicions after this thing is over with. No loose ends. This isn't a simple matter of killing Horn. My people are vulnerable to suspicion. They want no questions asked of them afterward."

Ben Toy smiled at the lawyer's answer. He slid over closer to Wynn. He put his arm around the pin-striped suit. This was where he earned all his pay.

"Then I think we've had enough Looney Tunes for tonight," he said in a soft, Texas drawl. "You owe us half of our money as of right now. You have the money inside your jacket."

Wynn tried to pull away, "I was told I'd get to talk with Berryman himself," he protested.

"You just give me the money you're supposed to have," Toy said. "The money or I leave. No more talk."

The southern man hesitated, but he finally took out the brown envelope. The contact was completed.

Ben Toy walked away with fifty thousand dollars stuffed around his dungarees. He was feeling very good about himself.

Over his head the City Hall clock sounded like it was floating in the sky. *Bongg. Bongg. Bongg.*

Inside the pub window Thomas Berryman was clicking off important photographs of Harley John Wynn.

The Thomas Berryman Number had begun.

About the Author

JAMES PATTERSON is one of the best-known and biggest-selling writers of all time. Since winning the Edgar™ Award for Best First Novel with *The Thomas Berryman Number*, his books have sold in excess of 300 million copies worldwide and he has been the most borrowed author in UK libraries for the past seven years in a row. He is the author of some of the most popular series of the past decade – the Alex Cross, Women's Murder Club, Detective Michael Bennett and Private novels – and he has written many other number one bestsellers including romance novels and stand-alone thrillers. He lives in Florida with his wife and son.

James is passionate about encouraging children to read. Inspired by his own son who was a reluctant reader, he also writes a range of books specifically for young readers. James is a founding partner of Booktrust's Children's Reading Fund in the UK.

THE *SUNDAY TIMES* BESTSELLER

14th Deadly Sin

James Patterson
& Maxine Paetro

**A new terror is sweeping the streets of San Francisco.
And the killers look a lot like cops...**

As Detective Lindsay Boxer investigates whether the perpetrators are brilliant impostors or police officers gone rogue, she receives a chilling warning to back off.

On the other side of the city, an innocent woman is murdered in broad daylight in front of dozens of witnesses. But there are no clues and no apparent motive.

With killers in disguise, a maniac murderer on the loose, and danger getting ever closer to Lindsay's door, could this be one case too many for the Women's Murder Club?

CENTURY

Hope to Die

James Patterson

I am alone, I thought. Alone.

Pain knifed through my head. I sank to my knees, bowed my head, and raised my hands towards heaven.

'Why?' I screamed. 'Why?'

Detective Alex Cross has lost everything and everyone he's ever cared about.

His enemy, Thierry Mulch, is holding his family hostage. Driven by feelings of hatred and revenge, Mulch is threatening to kill them all, and break Cross for ever.

But Alex Cross is fighting back.

In a race against time, he must defeat Mulch, and find his wife and children – no matter what it takes.

THE END-GAME HAS BEGUN.

CENTURY

Invisible

James Patterson
& David Ellis

My nightmare: it's the same every time. I'm trapped in my bedroom with an inferno blazing around me.

It started eight months ago, when my sister was killed in a house fire. Her death was written off as an accident, but I know she was murdered.

There have been dozens of 'accidental' fires across the US over the past year that are all too similar to be coincidental.

I've never been more sure of anything.

One of the worst serial killers of all time is being ignored.

And it's up to me to stop him.

arrow books

THE *SUNDAY TIMES* BESTSELLER

Burn

James Patterson
& Michael Ledwidge

**Detective Michael Bennett is coming home to New York.
And a world of unimaginable evil awaits.**

Having brought an end to the vengeful mission of the ruthless
crime lord who forced the Bennett family into hiding, Michael is
finally back in New York City.

However, Bennett is thrust straight back into a horrifying case: a
witness claims to have seen a group of well-dressed men holding
a sickeningly depraved and murderous gathering in a condemned
building.

The report reads like the product of an overactive imagination.
But when a charred body is found in that very same building, the
unbelievable claim becomes all too real...

CENTURY

NYPD Red 3

James Patterson
& Marshall Karp

A chilling conspiracy leads NYPD Red into extreme danger.

Hunter Alden Jr. has it all: a beautiful wife, a brilliant son and billions in the bank. But when his son goes missing and he discovers the severed head of his chauffeur, it's clear he's in danger of losing it all.

The kidnapper knows a horrific secret that could change the world as we know it. A secret worth killing for. A secret worth dying for.

New York's best detectives, Zach Jordan and Kylie MacDonald, are on the case. But by getting closer to the truth, Zach and Kylie are edging ever closer to the firing line . . .

CENTURY

ROMANCE
Sundays at Tiffany's (*with Gabrielle Charbonnet*) •
The Christmas Wedding (*with Richard DiLallo*) •
First Love (*with Emily Raymond*)

FAMILY OF PAGE-TURNERS

MIDDLE SCHOOL BOOKS
Middle School: The Worst Years of My Life (*with Chris Tebbetts*) • Middle School: Get Me Out of Here! (*with Chris Tebbetts*) • Middle School: My Brother Is a Big, Fat Liar (*with Lisa Papademetriou*) • Middle School: How I Survived Bullies, Broccoli, and Snake Hill (*with Chris Tebbetts*) • Middle School: Ultimate Showdown (*with Julia Bergen*) • Middle School: Save Rafe! (*with Chris Tebbetts*)

I FUNNY SERIES
I Funny (*with Chris Grabenstein*) •
I Even Funnier (*with Chris Grabenstein*) •
I Totally Funniest (*with Chris Grabenstein*)

TREASURE HUNTERS SERIES
Treasure Hunters (*with Chris Grabenstein*) •
Treasure Hunters: Danger Down the Nile (*with Chris Grabenstein*)

HOUSE OF ROBOTS
House of Robots (*with Chris Grabenstein*)

HOMEROOM DIARIES
Homeroom Diaries (*with Lisa Papademetriou*)

KENNY WRIGHT
Kenny Wright: Superhero (*with Chris Tebbetts, to be published May 2015*)

MAXIMUM RIDE SERIES

The Angel Experiment • School's Out Forever •
Saving the World and Other Extreme Sports •
The Final Warning • Max • Fang • Angel •
Nevermore • Forever (*to be published May 2015*)

CONFESSIONS SERIES

Confessions of a Murder Suspect (*with Maxine Paetro*) •
Confessions: The Private School Murders (*with Maxine
Paetro*) • Confessions: The Paris Mysteries (*with
Maxine Paetro*)

WITCH & WIZARD SERIES

Witch & Wizard (*with Gabrielle Charbonnet*) •
The Gift (*with Ned Rust*) • The Fire (*with Jill
Dembowski*) • The Kiss (*with Jill Dembowski*) •
The Lost (*with Emily Raymond*)

DANIEL X SERIES

The Dangerous Days of Daniel X (*with Michael Ledwidge*)
• Watch the Skies (*with Ned Rust*) •
Demons and Druids (*with Adam Sadler*) • Game Over
(*with Ned Rust*) • Armageddon (*with Chris
Grabenstein*)

GRAPHIC NOVELS

Daniel X: Alien Hunter (*with Leopoldo Gout*) •
Maximum Ride: Manga Vols. 1–8 (*with NaRae Lee*)

For more information about James Patterson's novels, visit
www.jamespatterson.co.uk

Or become a fan on Facebook